OUT OF EMPIRE

Out of Empire

A novella

by

CHRISTOPHER ASLAN OVERFELT

Adelaide Books
New York / Lisbon
2021

PART 1: NORTH AMERICA

Chapter 1

Just outside of Hermosa, South Dakota, a double wide trailer with a gravel parking lot sits along highway 40. A sign with a flashing arrow points towards the trailer, and on most evenings there a few cars and trucks in the lot. One of them belongs to Splint.

There is a little screened in area out front of the trailer, and then two slanted steps lead inside. A small dance floor sits in the corner, behind a few tables and a row of electronic slot machines. There is a kitchen in the back and a bar in front that is stocked with coolers full of beer.

When the bartender comes out of the kitchen, she sees Splint sitting alone at the bar. She takes a beer from a cooler and sets it before him, opening the top with an audible snap.

Let me know if you need anything else, honey, she says.

He doesn't. He sits and drinks, and stares blankly into the screen of the little television that hangs over the bar, showing a nightly newscast. After a while, an old gambler at the slots comes to the bar and sits next to Splint.

How's working with Larry going? he asks him.

Splint shrugs his shoulders.

Have you had a day off in the last month?

Splint shakes his head.

How many hours a day are you working?

Putting his finger on his chin, Splint thinks for a minute, and says, I worked fourteen hours today.

The gambler laughs.

I can't believe that man is fifty five years old and still works the way he does.

The next morning, Splint works in the depths of a metal fabrication shop. Black dust lies on everything like a grimy coat. As Larry applies the heat of a torch to a stubborn nut, Splint turns it with a wrench. Only he doesn't. He fumbles slightly, and misses the flats of the nut. Larry shuts off the torch and looks down at him.

You have to turn it while the metal is hot, he says. Otherwise it won't work.

When they get the nuts loose, and remove the broken plate from the frail cutter, they weld a new one in place. Splint crouches over the metal, gun in hand, and lays a bead along the lap joint. When he finishes, he raises his mask and inspects his weld, a uniform line of steel waves cresting gently one after the other. Larry stands over his shoulder.

I told you to do three inch welds with three inch spaces, he says.

Splint looks down at the metal, which is slowly discoloring from red to blue, and then looks up at Larry.

Do you want me to redo it?

I want you to pay attention to what you're doing.

By midmorning, Splint is in the cab of a tractor, listening to the hum of the big tires rolling on the pavement of a two lane highway. Through the glass, he watches the countryside pass by, an unravelling tableau of rotting wood and weed trees, bare foundations and empty frame houses. He sees, swirling up the branches of a black locust, the structure of a barn, its shingles and siding spread like leaves around the fingers of the tree. And then it passes by and is gone.

Among the slanted stalks of corn, he pulls the frail cutter behind the tractor. The blades of the cutter spin, and the silage is left chopped and brown in his wake. The field in which he works has no visible end, no perimeter toward which he can progress, no horizon which is not defined by the slender shapes of cut corn stalks. And so Splint sails his vessel in a sea of solitude.

At some point in the day, Splint stops the tractor, and in the deafening silence of a fallow field, lets a loud stream of piss splash onto the soil. He directs the stream onto a shortened corn stalk, on the pulp of which sits a black butterfly that flutters its wings and flies away.

As the sun sets behind a wall of black clouds in the west, Splint sees a pair of headlights in the distance. In the deepening dusk, the headlights brighten and dim, rise and fall, as the truck crosses the field towards him. He watches as it approaches, and, when it comes close, he watches Larry step out. He sighs and turns off the tractor.

There is a stiff wind, now, and the white feather of hair on Larry's head stands straight up. He stands with his hands in his pockets, braced against the suddenly cold wind.

Never shut off the tractor with the PTO still engaged, says Larry, as Splint walks towards him.

But the noisy wind takes his words and Splint doesn't hear him. Or maybe he doesn't want to. They walk around the tractor together, to where the frail cutter rests on the ground, and Larry leans into the wind to shout in Splint's ear.

Did you check the oil in the gearbox?

Now the loose corn silage from the field has begun to pick up and carry in the wind, projectiles that swirl and blow against the tractor and the two men. Above the blades on the frail cutter is a gearbox, the fill cap of which Larry unscrews, and a blast of smoke bursts from the opening, along with the stench of burnt metal.

I can't believe you ran this fucking thing all day with no oil in the gearbox, he says.

But the words make no sound in the maelstrom. He makes a fist and then throws his thumb out towards the black sky, looking with murderous eyes at Splint.

Get it back to the shop!

When Splint gets home that night, the wind has not abated, in fact it has strengthened, and his little trailer rocks and groans from the stress as he enters. There is only an empty shell to greet him. He sheds his clothes and lies on a couch, exhausted. He tries to think of things, but there is nothing in his mind, only an aching tiredness. What day is it? He doesn't know. Probably Tuesday or Wednesday. What difference does it make, when everyday is the same?

As he listens to the howl of wind, his mind drifts back to his time at Minot Air Force Base up in North Dakota. He had been an aircraft mechanic there, and now he wishes he could call his old friends and tell them where he is and what he is doing. His loneliness suffocates him.

The din outside the trailer grows louder, as if suddenly there were a train passing directly next to it. What would it be to die? Death would be better than the suffering, he thinks. It is the suffering before death that is frightening. When you're dead, you don't know it. There can be no pain after death.

And then Splint feels a sudden rush of wind, as the glass in his kitchen window is shattered. His trailer is torn from its slab foundation, rolling across the earth like a pinwheel spinning in a gale.

Chapter 2

In the soft bottom land of the river valley, Phlox cradles a thousand cabbage seeds in their palm. The seeds are smooth red beads that run easily through their fingers. Rearing back their arm, Phlox flings forth their hand and lets the seeds silhouette like rain on the sky. They scatter across the land as a strong wind carries them off. And who can say which of those seeds will find conditions favorable to their desire, and which will lie in the earth, awaiting their time to flourish?

Suddenly Phlox is running through the grass as hail pummels the earth. When they reach the shed, they watch a cloud descend and walk across the plain like a man. It picks up the earth, the trees and the roots, and with heavy arms throws them through the air.

After the tornado has passed, the plain is sheathed in a layer of ice like glass. Phlox sees their belgian shepherd running across the land, and they take off to follow her.

Windy! they call out to the dog. Windy!

They find Windy down by the river, sitting at the base of a cottonwood tree. Behind the tree, the river is broad and coiled in the land, carrying the color of the mottled sky on its back. Phlox looks up into the high canopy of tree limbs, and sees a trailer home stabbed through with branches. From the broken floor of the trailer, they can just see Splint's leg dangling in the air.

Phlox climbs the tree, and manages to get inside the trailer where Splint lies semi-conscious. They kneel over him and examine his condition.

I'm going to get a ladder and a rope, they say, and get you down.

Splint lifts his head and looks around him.

Where's Larry? he says.

I don't know, says Phlox. I don't know Larry.

Good.

Beneath a blistering afternoon sun, Splint stands with his tennis shoes buried in the crawling vines of a cucumber plant. Not just one plant, but hundreds, arranged in rows across the plain. He places his feet carefully, bending down to grasp the long shaft of a cucumber, and plucks it from the vine. Phlox stands just down the row from him, picking. Windy lies in the shade.

How's the knee doing? Phlox asks him.

Which one? says Splint.

The one that almost got skewered by a tree branch.

Oh. It's fine, just sore.

I never thought I'd find a person in the top of a tree.

I never thought there'd be enough people in that little town to eat this many cucumbers.

Just wait till we get to the sweet potatoes.

They harvest cucumbers throughout the long afternoon, and then they wash and pack them in the shade of a big cotton-wood tree. In the big tub of water, their hands swim among the cukes like clean, pale fish. They bring them dripping out of the water and pack the cukes into boxes.

How long has your family been on this land? says Splint.

A long time, says Phlox. The first nations came across the siberian pass over ten thousand years ago. This place is special to us. It's something we feel very strongly about, something to be protected and taken care of. What about you? How'd you come out to black hills country?

I was a mechanic in the military up in Minot, North Dakota. I got out and got a job with a farmer down here. He did row crops, corn and soybeans. Thousands of acres of it. We harvested corn for three weeks straight, twelve hours a day, every day. No weekends. It got to the point that I didn't know what day it was. When I slept, all I saw was corn.

You don't want to work for him anymore?

No. He was a real asshole. I think that twister might have done me a favor.

Throughout the summer, Splint's days are filled with brown dirt as he works on Phlox's farm. A fine dust picks up in the wind and blows across the hills. It settles on his boots, his clothes, and skin. And his skin becomes sun boiled, the color of a burnt potato. Down rows of new growth, the blade of his hoe cuts cleanly into the soil. His hands work lightly the shaft, the smooth wood grain wearing to callouses the web of his thumbs and pads of his fingers.

And when the rain comes, it crashes down in egg sized droplets, exploding and slaking the thirst of the dry earth. Splint and Phlox run together across the plain, the rain beating down upon them. In the shed, they peel the clinging fabric from their skin, as the rain pummels the tin roof. Their bodies clash, shuffling against one another, a discordant rhythm of clenched flanks and twisted torsos. They slouch together against the shed wall when their energy is spent.

When are you going to tell me why you're really here? says Phlox, still clutching a fistfull of Splint's hair.

I'm a murderer, says Splint. That's why I'm here.

Who did you murder?

It was an accident. I was an aircraft mechanic in the military. I made a mistake, and the airplane crashed.

That isn't murder, Splint.

They charged me with manslaughter because I had alcohol in my blood when the plane went down.

Did you go to jail?

No. I ran. I was afraid of going to prison. I came down here to hide out. That's when I got a job with Larry. And then the wind brought me to you.

Phlox leans against Splint, and they listen to the heavy rainfall on the shed. After awhile, Phlox speaks over the rain.

How many people has the American military murdered? they say.

What are you talking about? says Splint.

I'm talking about my people, the Lakota. How much has been lost for the sake of your empire?

My empire? I don't own anything. I'm a fucking fugitive. And besides, it's your empire too.

Is it?

In late summer, they dig up the sweet potatoes together beneath a lead gray sky. Splint's pitchfork sinks into the mounded earth like teeth into tender meat, turning up the soil. As they come to the surface, the sweet potatoes are blood red, like newborn piglets in the dirt. Phlox takes the nest of tubers and tears them from the vine, and then throws them in the wheelbarrow.

And then the frosts come, and the leaves turn sick, and all that remains standing in the fields are the crowns of broccoli, bright green like new grass. Phlox's knife slices through the thick stalks, cutting the heads and tearing off the leaves. Splint wears gloves and leans into the bitter wind to toss the heads of broccoli into a box.

I'm thinking of going further south, he says. I'm not going to stay here through the winter.

Murder and travel are the oldest of human traits, says Phlox. I never expected you to stay.

Chapter 3

In his truck, Splint lies across the bench seat in a sleeping bag. On a nightly basis now, he wakes up in a panic attack. Someone is yelling, but when he looks out the window of his truck, there is only the empty night. The weight of a belgian shepherd is curled on his legs. He scratches her behind the ear, his palm on her head.

Windy, he says.

He drives on. In towns unknown, he watches faces stretch and warp into hideous caricatures. The masks repeat again and again. In a park, he brushes snow from a bench seat. The snow has begun to melt beneath the midday sun. From the trestle of an empty swing set, icicles drip cold water. Windy sniffs at a paper wrapper buried in the snow.

The little town's main street is paved with red brick, and the empty storefronts still wear signs that point to boarded windows and chained doors. Above the naked branches of the trees, the clock of a courthouse strikes eleven. Splint kicks along the tracks of a train yard, where the coal cars stand silent and hollow. He throws a rock at a bulging belly, and it rings across the silent day. Windy chases its echo.

As he drives further south, the snow turns to rain, and then to overcast sky. In Coronado, Kansas, the fragile skin of the earth begins to break and tear, protrusions of rock lifting the grass like a skirt. And from the tears come rocks that spire upward in wind carved sculptures, landmarks defining an uncertain path into anxiety.

Ascending a summit, from the top of which he can see the land descending around him almost imperceptibly, his truck dies. The silence atop that peak is startling. Against the frame of the truck, the wind whistles through the porous quarter panels. Splint stands at the opened hood and examines the engine.

An inline four cylinder, mounted longitudinally. A simple design, effective and efficient. Fuel, air, compression, spark. Could be a head gasket. Two hundred thousand miles. Ten years now. I bought this truck when I was fifteen years old. Distributor, maybe. No spark.

You're out of gas.

Splint looks down at Windy, sitting beside him.

What?

You're out of gas, she says.

They walk for many empty miles, finally coming to a cattle feedlot. The smell staggers them. In the cold mud, the cattle trample the earth, stirring the dead soil and dung with heavy hoofs. Their massive skulls hang between steel tubing, feeding in the never ending grain troughs.

Poor cows, says Windy.

You're going to have to stop talking to me, says Splint. Or people are going to think I'm crazy.

They pass each heavy head, watching the wide nostrils, the bulbous eyes, the masticating jaws the size of a grown man's elbow. Aside from the cattle, the place is empty. Around them, the feedlot expands like a brown smudge on the land, mud pits divided with heavy metal fencing, the earth torn and fruitless for miles.

They follow the narrow corridors through the herds, winding channels narrowed to traffic cattle in and out of corrals. In the distance, above the chutes and fencing, the tall silos stand like towers, out from which a set of railroad tracks divides the lot. Hopping a gate and a few squeeze chutes, they climb onto the apron of a rail car and warm themselves in the sun.

And then Splint falls asleep. He sleeps for a long time, and dreams of walking across the llano estacado, a spotless pan of dry grass and dusty soil. Before him, two iron tracks unspool across the faultless plain, slick with moonlight. He follows the railroad ties until he sees a hollow flame out in that darkness.

He approaches slowly, and sees around the flame two faces, one old and one young. As the faces talk, fat slabs of meat hiss on spits over the fire. Splint crouches down and listens to them.

Why are you here? asks the young face.

I came here from a place across the world, says the old face. It was a place filled with sickness, corruption, and greed. I grew up blind to its disease, because I was sick with it, too. And then I found something, and it showed me what it was to live a life of freedom. They were letters written on a page, dead ink and pulp that were endowed with a creative force that shook me to my core.

The old face looks up into the sky, and then goes on.

And I knew, then, that the ways of men and women were flawed, and that I could not escape them, because, indeed, I am a man, too. But this land is different. This land is a new beginning for flawed humankind, and the world that will be established here will be ordained by God, and it will be beautiful.

I am just a child, says the young face, and even I can hear the hypocrisy in your words.

You are referring to the leader of men and women. His ways are the old ways. The way of violence and power, of corruption and greed. It is true that we have brought our flawed ways with us to this land. But there is another leader of men and women who is different, and who will teach us on this new land how to live in peace and humility and forgiveness.

These ideas you preach, says the young face, are not foreign to this land, or to its people. We know corruption and greed, and we know love and forgiveness. And your culture does not run any deeper than ours. What then, is the cost you are willing to pay for this shiny new kingdom? And how much are you willing to compromise to nestle into the arms of power?

The old man pauses for a moment, and watches the hollow flame boil. Then he speaks.

What you have done here, to draw Coronado's army away from your people and into confusion, is a story that will be told as long as there are people on this plain. Your name will be carried in reverence by your people.

But there will be another story told, and it, too, will live on in this land. It will take root in the soil and it will change the color of this grass to a blood red. And the cities of men and women that are built upon this plain will take the name of the leader of men, and he, too, will be held in reverence.

And these two narratives will coexist on this plain, one among your people, and one among mine. One is a narrative of the subversion of power, and the other speaks of its triumph. There will be a hundred years, two hundred years, three hundred years, four hundred years, five hundred years, and while the narrative of power blooms like a thousand flowers in the sun, the narrative of its subversion will lie seeded in the soil, awaiting its time to flourish.

Chapter 4

Splint wakes to a biting cold, an ache that leaves his core shaking. A strong wind whips his face, and a jolting piece of metal thrusts itself into his back. It takes him a moment to recognize that the train he is on is now moving. Through the metal grate next to him, the bulbous eye of a cow watches him.

Sitting up, he can see that the sun is shining like a red rubber ball. It now shines upon a land of red rock carved into deep canyons and high mesas. Splint lets the sun shine on his face, warming him. It is an exhilarating feeling. Exhilarating, too, is the view, as Splint peers over the apron of the rail car and sees nothing but a sheer rock face, descending into nothingness. A clean canyon, streaked with ribbons of purple and yellow strata, rises above and falls below.

How long have I been asleep? he says.

Windy is curled in the corner of the apron. She doesn't answer. The train carries on, out of the canyon, onto a plateau where dark scrub grows from the shallow soil. Painted hills fold together in the distance. Splint watches the sun rise, and at noon, its full warmth is upon him, even heating the steel on which he sits. And then he grows conscious of his stomach, a desolate howling within himself.

In the evening, the train slows atop an empty mesa. For a long time, it rolls slowly, until it feels as if there is no motion. Splint looks around, but there is no structure or road to indicate life, only the long land and short scrub. He climbs down off the train and begins to walk. Windy follows him. Before he leaves the train, he opens the doors of the rail cars to release the cattle.

They walk southward long into the night, hoping to find a road. Instead, they find a copper mine. Among the spires of wind blown canyons, the earth descends into a deep pit of stripped rock and hidden ore. The moon shines a grotesque light down into the bowels of the earth. They follow the pit road down, until the shovel of an excavator rears up into the light like some kind of leviathan.

Climbing onto the tracks, Splint opens the plexiglass door of the excavator and gets inside. He holds the door open for Windy. The cab provides shelter from the desert cold, and in the cup holder beside the operator's seat, he finds a bag of peanuts and a styrofoam cup of cold coffee. He lets Windy lap up a splash of coffee, and gives her a few peanuts to eat.

What do you think? he says.

About what? says Windy.

I don't know, riding a train and being cold and hungry.

I've been in better situations.

Me too.

In the morning, he is roused awake by a man opening the plexiglass door.

Gotta get out, says the man.

Where am I? says Splint.

Are you serious?

No. No, I'm not.

He and Windy take the long road up out of that hole, the big trucks now screaming by, carrying their loads of heavy soil.

Halfway up, one of them stops, its passenger side window rolled down. From the driver's seat, a woman motions to Splint.

Need a ride?

Splint opens the big door of the truck, and Windy jumps in, and then he climbs up into the seat. The heavy door jars against the frame as it shuts, slightly off center on its sagging hinges.

Who's this? says the driver, laying a heavy hand on Windy's head.

This is Windy, says Splint.

Hi Windy. My name's Mary.

The truck shakes as the power of the diesel engine is sent through the clutch and gears of the transmission and back to the transaxle. Splint watches the woman as she shifts the big rig through the gears, and only when he looks across the seat does he notice she only has one arm.

They tried to tell me I couldn't drive a truck, she says. Not because I've got one arm but because I'm a woman.

Splint and Windy bump along in the seat beside her, as the black asphalt unrolls on that red land before them. The road meanders between the high walls of canyons, and out onto sun drenched plateaus, spotted with horned antelope grazing on the thorn scrub. On one distant peak, Splint sees a wild ram climbing on a ledge, the walls of which could have been sculpted on a potter's wheel.

I used to have a truck just like this, says Splint.

Oh ya?

No. Not really. It was a little Nissan pickup.

What happened to it?

It ran out of gas.

Mary looks at Splint with heavy lidded eyes.

If you need help, all you have to do is ask, she says.

The narrow road is covered with dust, and as it winds among the stunted juniper and cactus, the pavement can hardly be discerned from the soil. No cars disturb the dust, and only the mining trucks pass occasionally.

As the ridged hills rise in steep cliffs above them, little scarves of snow can still be seen in the upper echelons of rock. A little ravine opens up alongside the road, in the bottom of which runs a gray band of water. As the water follows the road, its path begins to widen, and play among the shelved landings, splashing in falls from drop to drop. Its color transforms from yellow in the shallows to green and then dark blue in its depths. A few speckled trout hang motionless in the pools, as if encased in gelatin.

In a cleared space in the scrub, Splint sees a group of people singing together. The group wears bright clothing, a vision that stands out among the dusty scrub and dry soil. Behind them, a wall of rock ascends into the sky, wrinkled by erosion and colored with sulphur and lime.

Who's that? Splint asks.

Mary looks out the window, but the vision has passed, and she looks back down the long straight ribbon of road. Later, at a diner alongside the highway, Splint and Windy climb down out of the truck. He holds a few dollars in his hand. Mary leans over the seat to look down at him.

Take care of that dog, she says.

Thanks for the ride, says Splint. And for the cash.

Inside the diner, he eats at a square table, upon which a plastic tablecloth crinkles lightly. He lets the sun warm him through the window. Beneath the table, Windy's tail flops quietly on the carpet.

As he finishes his meal, he sees through the window a procession passing by on the highway. It seems to be the same group of people that were singing in the desert, all travelling on foot. It takes a long time for them to pass, and Splint wonders who they might be, and what bonds of kinship have brought them to this place.

When the waitress comes around to refill his coffee, he places his hand over the cup.

I'm ready for the check, he says.

Chapter 5

Beneath a hazy winter sun, a group of people gather together in the desert. They link hands, and sing songs. Their song radiates outward, filling the quiet air around them. Their voices settle like dust upon the ocotillo, upon the small red blossoms that grace the desert. In the water, their voices swim like fish from pool to pool, ripple to ripple.

Behind them, a sheer rock face rises into the sky, and their song climbs its walls and leaps magnificently into the air. When it lands, and the song ends, a woman steps out from the group and speaks to them. She talks about trauma, about erased identities. How do you navigate a world without a past? How do you raise children with no knowledge of yourself?

We are all wounded, she says. And by protecting these waters, we can begin the journey towards healing.

Wendsler stands among the group, and when his daughter finishes speaking, he takes her in his arms.

You did great, baby, he says.

The group disperses, and Wendsler gets in his dusty car and drives off across the desert landscape. It is a big car, an old Lincoln Mark Eight, and it sways luxuriously beneath him on its heavy suspension. In place of a radio, he hums a song and drums his thumbs on the steering wheel. Housed in the dash, behind the steering wheel, is a coolant gage, the needle of which begins to rise.

The needle has swung into the red by the time Wendsler sees it, and he quickly pulls onto the shoulder and turns off the car. Beneath the propped up hood, he leans over the engine and listens to the boiling coolant, rumbling like a ghost within the radiator hose. Beyond the car, on the shoulder of the road, he sees a man and a dog walking towards him.

When Splint and Windy come up to the side of the car, Wendsler is still leaning over the engine bay. He tells Splint that the engine is overheating, and, from a small tool kit in the trunk, Splint takes a ratchet and a ten millimeter socket and removes the thermostat. He holds the hot metal, scalding in his palm.

This is what lets the coolant flow out of the engine, and into the radiator, says Splint. Sometimes it gets stuck closed and won't let the coolant flow through, and the engine overheats.

Splint bolts the empty housing back onto the engine, and then pours water from a bottle into the radiator. As they ride in the car together, Splint asks Wendsler where he's at.

You don't know where you're at? says Wendsler.

I've just been walking for a few days. I guess I'm a little lost.

This is the San Carlos Apache reservation, says Wendsler.

At a little gas station with a garage, Wendsler buys Splint and Windy a sandwich, and they sit on the hood of his car beneath the desert sun and eat them. It is a wide hood, the flat kind from the old cars in the nineties, and they sit with their feet propped up on the bumper.

I was wondering who those people were down at the springs, says Splint.

The Apache people believe that those waters are sacred, says Wendsler. They are blessed with healing spirits by the Creator.

The mining company wants to dig beneath the springs, and we're trying to stop them.

Splint pulls the long tendril of an onion from his sandwich. The curled ribbon is translucent white with a layer of purple skin, and he pinches the crisp flesh in his fingernails. Then he inhales its tangy odor and eats it.

How far is the border from here? he asks.

It's about a three hour drive south, says Wendsler. But I can't take you any farther.

Splint and Windy leave Wendsler, and follow the springs up into the mountains. At first, the grade is shallow, a gradual ascent that is hardly noticeable. The water widens out around gravel shoals with steep canyon walls on either side. The rock face is smooth, cut in even lines that intersect one another in geometric patterns. The sun plays on the angles in light and shadow.

Rising out of the canyon, the water turns up the hillside, falling from rock to rock, shaded with green saplings of birch and oak. Splint and Windy stop where the water cascades down a sheer rock face, pooling in a shallow bowl of limestone.

Should we get in?

Windy looks up at Splint.

It'll be cold.

Splint sheds his clothes, spreading them out on the branches of a willow tree. The musty fabric carries his odor, the damp musk of unwashed skin filtering around the little grove. He stands in the pool, letting the ice cold water prick his ankles. His chest constricts, and he fights for breath, and then all at once he plunges into the pool. For a moment, the water encases him, clenching him in its grasp.

Beneath the surface, his existence takes on a different meaning. Time flows away, and there is only the water and the rock and the light and the shadow. It is a world shorn of its outer shell, like a tortoise exposing its soft belly to him. And, indeed, Splint sees a turtle darting through the murk, the sunlight just catching the shallow ridges of its shell.

He climbs from the water, and warms himself in the sun, and then they continue on up the mountain. The spruce and fir begin to grow up out of the cracked rock, and then the tall forests of pine take hold, furring the folded ridges with their soft needles. The water now seeps down the rock face, streaking it with rust and slicking its surface. And then it disappears altogether.

At night, they find a dark hole in the hillside in which to sleep. In that womb of rock, Splint thinks over his decisions.

Maybe this was a mistake, he says.

What's that? says Windy.

Coming into the mountains, alone.

Of all your decisions, this is the one you question?

Windy lays her head on Splint's lap, and tells him a story.

There was a dog, long ago, she says, lost upon the plain. She was without a name, and she was cold and lonely. In a matter of hours, a cold wind had brought a blanket of snow that held the level land like a blank white slate, and it lay on her back, too. And when the night came there was no moon or stars, and she had no way to guide herself on that frozen tundra. She was lost. Her nose could find no food and her feet no warmth.

Even among the legs of the bison, she could find no relief from the bitter cold in their shaggy coats, and so she left the herds behind. And there was a hunting party of men that were following the herds, and she crept quietly into their camp and she snuck beneath the flap of a hide shelter and she crawled beneath a pile of hides to sleep.

In the morning, when the man in the shelter woke and picked up a buffalo robe to go outside, he saw the sleeping dog, so weak now she could not rise. And he opened the gut of a bison before her and she lapped the blood from the ground with her tongue. And then she slept again, and it was warm and good.

Where is your brother the coyote, and your cousin the fox, and your mother the wolf? the man asked her, and she told him that she had become lost and alone on the plain. And he gave her more meat to eat and she told him that she wanted to repay him for his kindness. But you are just a dog, said the man, and there is nothing a dog can do for a man but howl and keep him awake at night.

But she was strong and she told the men to pile their hides upon her back, and they did so, and the pile that she carried was so high that it reached to the heavens and the men were truly amazed. And not just the men of the earth, but a goddess in the sky, too, could see the tall pile from where she sat, and she stood and stepped down upon the hides and came to earth, and she blessed the dog with a litter of puppies.

And each man took a puppy and brought it to his wife and child and they rejoiced at the gift, and the people honored the dogs and the dogs honored the people.

Chapter 6

In the morning, they find a road that switchbacks along the ridge line, alongside which bare boulders are stacked in precarious pillars. From the bald hilltops, they can see down the long land below them, where the mountains slope into ravines, and the ridges rise like spines around their shallow bowls. In one pocket, far below, the water of a lake reflects the sunshine.

Throughout the day, a few cars pass them, but none stop. In the evening, just as Splint begins to panic, the lights of Tucson appear below him. They are warm and inviting in the lonely desert.

In Tucson, they sleep in a hostel with the money Wendsler gave them, but a drunk man in the bunk above them pisses in the bed, and Splint wakes up to the stale drip of urine. He and Windy leave the hostel and spend the night below a highway overpass, in the rafters of which a few other transients have camped.

One of them is named Orangepeel, and he shows Splint his rig, a bicycle leaning on its kickstand at the base of the concrete embankment. Attached to its frame is a little pull behind trailer, on the bed of which a radio is playing music. He and Splint circle the rig, admiring its handiwork.

This one here is a curtain rod, says Orangepeel. I attached it with a couple of c-clamps. I had it wedged with a piece of wood, but it come off on me in traffic.

This would be perfect for me and Windy, says Splint.

I can get you one.

I'll pay you, says Splint.

They take off across the city, and as the sun sheds its light on the desert streets, they come to a flea market embedded among the cactus and the scrub. Before a chain link fence, a long line of bicycles lean on one another, their wheels chained together.

When Splint picks one out, and pays for it, they ride together to the junkyard, where the scrap twists together in tangles of rust and debris. They find a few straight pieces for a frame, and an axle, and, with a few spare bicycle tires, Splint has a trailer to pull behind himself.

I had a tent, says Orangepeel. But I burned it down. I lit a candle that turned out to be a road flare. Damn thing nearly killed me.

Splint buys him lunch at a little cafe, and then they ride out upon the pavement, Splint's new rig rolling along beautifully. Windy sits on the rough wooden slats of the pull behind and lets the desert air run across her face, while Splint trundles through the gears of the ten speed. The traffic of the city winds around them, and soon thins out, and then there is just the long, lonely desert and a ribbon of pavement.

Orangepeel takes them to the aircraft boneyard, where the old shells of fuselages lie unwinged and rotting, like the skins of serpents shed in the desert. He pulls up a patch of loose chain link fence and they all duck through.

I used to work on that airplane, says Splint.

Orangepeel looks where Splint is pointing, and sees a high-tailed aircraft parked in a row of dozens of others just like it.

What is it? says Orangepeel.

It's a KC-135 refueler aircraft. You see that big boom on the back of it? That lowers down while the plane is in the air, and other airplanes can fly up to it and get fuel out of it.

No shit? You say you was a pilot?

No. I was just a mechanic.

But did you get to fly on them?

Ya, I did sometimes.

Where did you go?

All over the world. Wherever the military wanted me to go.

But you ain't in the military no more.

No, I'm not.

How come?

It's a long story.

You don't have to tell me. We've all got stories we don't want other people to know about.

As the sun begins to set, they climb into the empty hull of a C-5 Galaxy, an aircraft of unbelievable size and quality. The fuselage is open and gutted, picked clean of anything loose or extraneous. On all the ribs and spars is a thick scale, a virus of rust that eats like a cancer entire worlds of ferrous metals.

The space is quiet, cavernous. Lightning dances in blue streaks up and down the guts of the craft. Splint sits in the crevice of a bulkhead that protrudes from the darkness and rests. In his mind is a story told to him long ago of a man who once found refuge in the belly of a leviathan, and he wonders if there is a similar grace to be found here among these innards of steel. Because what is the sky but a reflection of those watery depths? And what are those creatures that find freedom from the land but the inheritors of those ancient bodies the move beneath us in the deep?

He sleeps, and in his dreams he writhes among a sea of serpents, and, indeed, when he wakes, just visible in the half light is a rattlesnake coiled in the hollow of a rib beside him. That unhooded eye peers out at him from the depths of its reptilian core, and they part ways as separate beings, whole and distinct.

Chapter 7

Splint and Windy ride out of Tucson, and in that rhythm of pavement and rubber and desert, there is a melody in his soul that sings itself to the world. At the perimeter of the world is the spine of a mountain that lies on the horizon like a sleeping dragon. Just above the ridge is a bank of clouds that carry a few streaks of lightning.

He sees nothing all day until a desert fox crosses his path, the tail of a lizard hanging from its snout. It doesn't wait for Splint to pass, but scurries out of sight. At some point in the day, two aircraft pass overhead, in formation, and the crackle of exhaust from their engines screams across the desert. They pass like demons into the ether.

That night, Splint and Windy sleep on the ground together, beneath a sky clear of any pollution. Lying in the dirt, Splint imagines the sky opened like a melon fruit, fat and dripping star light like juice. He imagines the light of galaxies dripping onto his face, honey sweet, tasting mildly citrus. He would lick that sky clean, until all that was left was a hollow rind, graying with daylight.

In the morning, they come into a little desert community, along the highway of which a few homes and businesses are scattered. Splint doesn't stop, but keeps pedalling, feeling the innervating morning air surge through his body. He takes a deep breath, and lets the warm sun cradle his shoulders.

The little two lane highway turns south, and after a while he sees a group of people gathered alongside the road. He slows down and watches them, and then comes to a stop where they are standing. A woman approaches his rig and kneels down to pet Windy.

Can I pet your dog? she says. She's gorgeous.

Go ahead. What is this place?

It's the border. Don't you know where you're at?

Oh ya. I guess I made it. What's going on out here?

Behind the group, a long wall stretches across the desert. Heavy construction equipment dozes the earth into wide swaths, and cranes lift the iron spars into place.

They're building a wall down here to stop migrants from coming across the border. They seized land illegally from the Tohono O'odham nation to build it. We're trying to raise awareness by protesting out here.

For a while, Splint watches a welder work at the construction site. The arc flashes from the hot iron in the bright desert sun. He thinks about his days welding in the shop with Larry, and feels a pang of longing in his hands for mechanical work.

As he admires the big truck on which the welding rig sits, he notices a uniformed agent among the construction workers. And then he notices more agents out along the perimeter of the site.

Suddenly the group is surrounded by armed men, and before anyone has a chance to say anything, they are placed in wrist restraints and led to a large van. The van is labeled with Border Patrol markings, and Splint turns to call out for Windy before he steps up on the bumper and into the cargo area. He doesn't see her, and the door is shut, and then he feels the van begin to roll out across the desert.

She'll be ok, says the woman next to him. We'll come back for her.

Thank you, says Splint. She's my best friend.

The members of the protest group are taken in for questioning, and then released. All except for Splint. His background check comes back with a warrant for involuntary manslaughter, and now he sits on a concrete floor, leaned back on a chain link fence. The Border Patrol facility is a big concrete warehouse divided into cells with chained fencing. Migrants push against the chainlink, swelling the cells with noise and desperation.

Splint finds another American in the cell, sitting on the ground next to two boys. He goes over and talks to him. His name is Randy.

How'd you get in here? says Splint.

Long story, says Randy. What about you?

I got rounded up with a protest group down at the border wall. I have warrants out, and now I'm stuck in here until the police come get me.

Randy turns and translates Splint's story to the two boys next to him, and they nod their heads in understanding. Then he turns back to Splint.

I found these two young men out in the desert, says Randy. It's very dangerous out there, and many people don't make it through. They almost didn't make it, themselves.

What happened to them?

Their scooter broke down in the desert. I picked them up on my motorcycle.

How did you find them?

It told you it was a long story.

I've got nothing but time, says Splint.

PART 2: CENTRAL AMERICA

Chapter 1

In Honduras, Randy walks next to the river. A little sandbar trails out of the woods and leads into the water. A couple of granite rocks jut from the earth. He ponders taking off his shoes and socks, and digging his toes into the sand. Maybe let the water run around his ankles. But then he thinks it would be unprofessional.

A few other men around him talk, and sometimes they stop, and one of them will say something to him. They wear jeans, with polo shirts tucked into their belts. They talk about concrete and access roads for heavy equipment. Randy squats down and thinks about the sand, and what kind of soil covers the mountain. He thinks about the rock that will be removed for the project.

They have lunch at a little roadside cafe. He has a plate of seafood from the coast and coffee. Out the window, he watches the trees move in the wind. A stand of oaks with a few pines. Along the road, trucks pass by, loaded with crates of mangoes and papaya. The birds in the trees are the color of lightning at night, and water in the sunshine.

They go over some paperwork, and look over a few plans. Randy gives his opinion on them.

My boss will send you the bill, he says as they shake hands.

When they leave the cafe, Randy drives out through the mountains alone. It is an enjoyable drive. He rolls down the window and lets the sounds and smells of the forest fill the car. Fresh pine fills the air.

Atop the high plateaus, the land is cleared into fields of short corn and sugar cane. A few men work in the cane with machetes. As Randy descends the mountain, the humidity picks up, and the trunks of the big oaks are wrapped in heavy moss. And the bright blooms of orchids trumpet their colors on long vines. The broad leaves of palms and ferns crowd the undergrowth.

He stops on a ridge, and looks out over the bowls of rolling forest. The mountains rise up beneath the green carpet like a spine beneath skin. In the evening, he finds the lights of the town strung along the mountain like lights on a tree. He stays in a little motel, and spends the night flipping channels on the television.

In the morning, he has breakfast at a little cafe. He eats chorizo and eggs, and sips coffee. He watches the waitress bustle in and out of the kitchen. The cafe opens out onto the square. On one end is a cathedral, and at the other end is a courtyard. A few people are gathered at the fountain, talking.

It is a sunny day, and Randy watches the sun shine on the brightly painted frescoes. The stucco facades are painted lime green and salmon colored pink. After breakfast, he walks through the market street, the stands filled with plantains and yams and onions and horseradish. The smell is piquant. Sitting on the tailgate of a truck, a woman watches him.

How long are you here for? she says.

Just a few days, says Randy. I work for a consulting firm. It's a business trip.

It's beautiful here, isn't it?

Very beautiful.

Our forests and rivers will capture your heart.

They already have.

Later in the day, he drives back out to the river. This time, he does remove his shoes and socks, and sinks his toes in the sand. A volcanic mix of sediment bathes his feet. There are a few others at the river. One man's name is Arturo. He is tall and lean, and wears a pair of shorts and sandals. He comes over to Randy, and stands next to him.

Are you here with the dam company? he says.

Randy shades his eyes to look up at him.

Yes, I am. How'd you know?

Arturo tells him that he's a lawyer working on behalf of the Lenca people.

We are trying to stop the construction of the dam, he says. The Lenca people depend on this water for their livelihoods.

I hadn't heard anything about it.

They go to a cafe together and talk. Arturo's office is just across the street. He has short hair that balds into a widow's peak, and he passes his hand across his head as he talks.

There's been a long history of international extractivism in this country, he says. The people want it to stop. They strip the land of its resources, leaving the people destitute. It started with the Spanish, hundreds of years ago. Now it's mainly international corporations, with the backing of the U.S. government.

I'm just a contractor, says Randy. I don't think most Americans know where Honduras is, honestly. My firm sends me down here periodically because I can speak Spanish. We never discuss politics about our business.

It's not political. It's basic ethics.

They eat fish caught from the river with rice and pickled onions. When they finish, Arturo shows Randy around his office.

How long are you staying? he says.

Just a few days, says Randy. I won't be staying long.

You should stop by tomorrow. I'll take you fishing on the river.

Thanks, says Randy. I will.

Chapter 2

In Tegucigalpa, Pilar goes around with his best friend Facile. Together, they explore the velvety dusks. Their feet feel the crevices
in the streets. They slant down the gutters in the rain soaked
hillsides. From the dimly lit doorways, the girls watch them,
their eyes as hard as rocks. They are filled with longings that
cannot be quenched, but can only fade with time, like lingering
coals in the dawn.

In the antiseptic light of a street lamp, Pilar and Facile
squat against a chain link fence. Below them, in the valley, the
city hums. The lights spread from a concentrated mass up into
the surrounding hills, and then disappear on the dark mountain
tops. They listen to the distant snarl of traffic.

We need a ride.

Yep.

In the washed up lees of an alley, they find an old Honda
c-90 scooter. It wears a heavy chain draped through its spokes,
locked to the leg of a gas meter.

It'll need some work.

I know how we can get some cash.

They go to a man's house, the front of which is guarded by
a high tin fence. Razor wire lines the balconies beneath the windows. Facile shouts something, and soon the tin fence opens,

revealing a gate. There is another boy standing there, shirtless in jean shorts, the threads of which dangle around his skinny legs.

We need a job.

And so, when they get paid for their errand, the boys buy bolt cutters, and the chain link holding the scooter in place pinches like taffy in its heavy jaws. Facile pushes the scooter down the street, its flat tires limping around the hubs. They take it to a garage around the corner, where an old man sits on a pile of tires, smoking. The creases in his fingers are lined with grease.

He looks at the scooter, and then sets it on its centerstand. He twists the throttle, watching the butterfly valve open and close in the little carburetor. The scooter is lime green, with a headlight that hangs down by a wire. He steps down on the kickstarter, feeling the piston run in the cylinder.

I'll put some new rings and a head gasket on it, he says. It ought to scream like a hornet.

How much will it cost? says Facile.

It will only take about an hour.

Ya, but how much will it cost?

How much do you have?

So they continue to run errands for the man, passing money mainly, some of which they get to keep. The scooter carries them wherever they need to go. The little two stroke motor screams between their legs, both of them squeezed together on the pillar seat. It zips down the hillside, kicking up dirt and gravel, Pilar clinging to the thin fabric of Facile's shirt, the collar of which tears at his neck.

At the bottom of the valley, the light suspension crunches the tires up into the fenders as they almost lose control on the asphalt avenue, the cars honking and swerving around them. A cop flips his lights, but has nowhere to go, as the traffic stalls.

Facile threads the needle, Pilar fisting sideview mirrors as they squeeze through the lanes like a rabbit through a snake.

They stay in an apartment in the valley. They don't know how to take care of themselves, much less a living space. They come and go at odd hours. Their neighbors watch them with a combination of wariness and contempt. They live with a man named Hector, who they learn to despise, but can't seem to shake.

On a balcony, they sit and watch Tegucigalpa. There is a little table between them, on the glass surface of which cold drinks sweat. A few palm and ceiba trees sprout from squares of dirt in the parking lot below. Across the way, a woman comes out onto a balcony and shakes a rug and then goes back inside.

Hector wants us to do a job, says Facile.

What kind? says Pilar.

The real kind.

I don't think I can do it.

I don't think we have to do anything. We just have to go with him.

Children play in the street below. Pilar watches them through the electrical wires that are strung in nests atop the light poles.

What if we say no?

You know what happens if we say no.

Before the hit job, Pilar visits his mother. Her name is Esda. She sits at the little kitchen table beneath a dim overhead light. With the shadows falling down her face, she looks old. For the first time in his life, Pilar sees her as a woman existing in a world of loss and love. His sister Asa sits across the table from her.

We are going back to the river, to the mountains, says Esda. You know we believe that river is sacred. It is worth fighting for.

I know, says Pilar.

You should come with us.

Pilar stands at the counter. He feels an adult pain, the anxiety of decision. Perhaps his first.

I don't want to leave Facile, he says.

Is he worth your life?

She stands, and presses against him. He feels good in her arms. Through his chest, she can feel his heartbeat. She is proud of him.

No matter what happens, she says, I love you. I brought you to Tegucigalpa when you were just a boy. The river was poisoned, and bringing you here saved your life. But now it is out of my hands. You must find out what is right, and what is wrong.

And so the next night, the boys ride up into the mountains in Hector's car. There are a few men with them, and it is an awkward, crowded ride. They smell of smoke and sour sweat. They roll down the windows to try to air out.

It should be an easy job, says Hector. It's about four hours away, in El Gueguecho.

Pilar shakes his head. The road winds through dense brush, the headlights thick with hard bodied insects. They thump on the windshield like rain. They pass little towns with one street light, the squares abandoned, the houses lightless in the night time.

On the high plateaus, the forest is clear cut into sheets of leveled land. Out in the night, the eyes of cattle glow like green orbs, rising and falling. The rows of sugarcane and corn pass like soldiers along the road. And then Pilar falls asleep.

Chapter 3

Randy wakes up in his little motel room. A strand of sunlight comes in through the curtains on the window. He lies in bed for a while, listening to the voices coming through the wall. He thinks about what he wants to eat for breakfast.

The bed lies low to the ground, and he can see himself in the dark television. He gets up and dresses. The sink in the bathroom is close to the toilet, and he brushes his teeth as he shits. When he goes outside, he tucks his button down shirt into his pants. The motel room opens onto an outdoor catwalk, and Randy can see another concrete building across the courtyard. He goes down the stairs, and then crosses the courtyard out to the parking lot, where his car is parked.

On his way out of town, he stops at Arturo's office. It's a little corner room in a strip mall. He goes through the glass door and comes to a desk. A woman sits in a chair behind it.

Is Arturo in? he asks.

She seems distracted. She doesn't look at him. She shakes her head.

He won't be in, she says. He's been...hurt.

He's been hurt?

Yes. He has been shot.

Is he ok?

I don't know. I don't think so.

Walking back outside, Randy blinks in the bright sunlight. He looks up and down the street, not quite sure what to do. He gets in his car and makes the long drive into Tegucigalpa. It takes four long hours, and it feels like four lifetimes.

When he comes into the city, he passes through the narrow neighborhoods, the houses of tin and concrete stacked roof to roof on the hillside. A few children kick a football in the street, and he slows to let them clear out. He passes a cathedral where stone spires rise at the corners, and votive candles gutter in the nave.

In the valley, the avenues widen out, shaded with tall palms. He drives through a long corridor of strip malls and gas stations, until he pulls into the parking lot of the car rental office. Inside, he turns in the keys to his rental car, and then he asks the woman behind the desk if she wants to look at the car. She looks out the door, and then looks back at him.

No. It's fine, she says.

He walks a little ways down the street, and finds a business with tall glass windows. Behind the glass are motorcycles leaning on their kickstands, and a salesman waving him in. He goes inside.

An hour later, he has a brand new motorcycle and a helmet to go with it. He calls his boss to tell him about the sudden change in plans.

Hey Ron, he says.

Hey Randy. How's the trip?

It's good. The plans look good. Listen, I'm gonna take a little extra vacation.

Oh ya?

Ya. I bought a motorcycle. I'm gonna ride it back.

From Honduras?

Ya.

There is a pause on the phone.

What'd you get?

A KTM 1200.

Nice.

Do you know anything about the dam company down here?

What do you mean?

I mean are they involved in any shady business practices?

What are you talking about, Randy?

Nothing. I'll talk to you when I get back.

He dons his helmet, and rides the bike out of Tegucigalpa. It hums beneath him like a happy cat. Above him, concealing the mountains, is a thunderstorm. Rain hangs down from the western sky like hair. He twists the throttle and lets the bike carry him through the heavy air, into the clouded future.

Chapter 4

Pilar's mother leaves Tegucigalpa, and goes back to the little town in the mountains. She rents a flat above an appliance repair shop, and on their first night there, she and Asa sleep together on the floor, exhausted. In the morning, at the breakfast table, they leave a place for Pilar. Esda thinks about how happy she would be just to see his face and hear his voice. When she goes out shopping, she thinks she sees him, and she follows him for a block or two. And then he disappears.

The next day, she does see him. In a little convenience store, he is standing, looking over a shelf of brightly wrapped candy bars. He doesn't look at all like what she had pictured. He looks tired. His chin is buried in a tuft of hair. When Pilar looks at her, she expects him to vanish. But he doesn't. He stands there solidly, stone faced.

Pilar, she says.

She takes him home. He sleeps for days. She puts up a curtain across the corner of the room for him, and he hardly leaves. After the third night of this, Asa wakes Esda up in the middle of the night. She is standing at the foot of the bed.

Mama, says Asa.

Esda sits up, and turns on the light.

What?

Pilar says he is sad.

Did you talk to him?

Yes.

And he talked to you?

Yes.

So Asa becomes Pilar's intercessor, and in a small way, his savior. She tells Esda what he wants to eat, and brings him his food. She plays with her dolls beside his pallet, and does her homework with him. She casts him as important characters in plots of her own devising. Pirates, robbers, school teachers. He wears silly hats for her.

Pilar is watching Asa color a picture when Facile shows up at the flat. Pilar sticks his head out through the curtain, and sees Facile standing awkwardly in the doorway. He puts on a pair of jeans, and then they go outside together. The stone street in front of the flat is narrow, with houses lining either side. The smells of a pastry shop come out from across the way.

I'm sorry I ran, says Pilar. I guess I didn't have the stomach for it.

That's ok, says Facile. I guess I didn't either.

The wind blows freely atop the mountain. A few plastic bags scratch in the street. Pilar and Facile watch them.

Hector set us up. They're going to pin that murder on us.

I know, says Pilar.

What should we do?

Asa comes out into the street. She holds to Pilar as if he were a kite that would blow away. They look off down the street, where the stone slopes into the forest that engulfs the world below.

I don't know, says Pilar.

That night, at the dinner table, Facile squeezes in between Asa and Pilar. They have fresh fish with beans and rice. Wild fruit lies halved in a bowl.

The man from downstairs caught the fish, says Esda. And Asa picked the fruit.

And I boiled the rice, too, says Asa.

We have to go, mama, says Pilar.

Where do you have to go?

They eat for a minute, and then Pilar says, Probably far away.

Are you in trouble, Pilar?

Yes, mama.

Chapter 5

So Pilar and Facile travel with a migrant caravan, headed north. There are men and women and children of every age with them. They are the poor, the hungry, and the drought stricken. We want jobs, they say. We want to feed our children. The group straggles in a long line along the shoulder of the highway, the electrical lines strung overhead.

Pilar and Facile let the women and children ride the scooter. It is waiting for them in the towns ahead. The nights are awkward. People sleep where they can, in parking lots and roadside grasslands. Some find rooms to stay in, some don't.

The people in the towns along the highway watch them. The group moves through the streets in the daytime, passing through the neighborhoods and businesses. They know why they are travelling. Some give them food, or let them wash their clothes and shower in their homes. Others ponder joining them.

At the Guatemalan border, a police force approaches them. The police line up on either side of the road, like some unholy gauntlet. They wear masks and vests, and carry metal batons. The caravan goes quiet. Some hesitate, not sure what to do. Pilar and Facile are the first to pass, and they flinch uneasily as the armed men gather around them. But the policemen stay calm, and the caravan passes through. The migrants breathe a little easier. They feel confident in the group they have gathered.

On a calm evening, Pilar and Facile eat grilled chicken from a street vendor and drink sweet milk. They sit on a curb and watch the little neighborhood around them. It could be the same neighborhood in which they grew up in Tegucigalpa. The same glassless windows, the painted concrete, the tin roof overhangs.

A man comes up and sits beside them. He is with the caravan and he wears a beard and tired eyes. Across the street, a few children wade in a concrete irrigation canal. He watches them, and then he speaks.

There is a rumor going around the caravan, he says.

Pilar and Facile look at him.

They say that maybe you two are running from something.

Of course we are, says Facile. Aren't you?

Yes. But we are not running from justice. We are running towards it.

Pilar and Facile are quiet, and they think for a minute.

They say that maybe you two were involved with the killing of a Lenca lawyer, says the man. A water protector. We are workers. Farmers and seamstresses. Teachers and carpenters. We cannot afford any extra baggage on our journey. You seem like good boys, but you have made your choices. We cannot endanger ourselves because of them.

And so they are marked. The next day, they leave the caravan, and take off on their own. On the scooter, they ride a narrow highway that sweeps along the green hills. Heavy vines climb from tree to tree, shrouding the mountains in dark foliage. The day passes uneventfully, until, in the afternoon, they realize they are lost.

As the twilight begins to dim the forest around them, they come to a goat standing in the road. He is big, and he stands head on before them. His thick horns roll back on his head. The drum brakes of the scooter squeal lightly as they come to a stop, and Pilar and Facile watch the goat.

Before they have time to react, it rears up on its hind legs and brings its horns down onto the headlight. It shatters into pieces, and then the goat takes off into the forest. Pilar and Facile sit atop the scooter, stunned.

I bet that goat belongs to somebody, says Pilar.

They follow the goat, stumbling down through sharp brakes of thorn scrub and ivy. They find a footpath that traces the bank of a creek. In a little clearing, they find a house, bordered with an empty corral. A little iron stove pipe pokes up through its tin roof. They squat on their heels and watch. From the open doorway comes an aroma of hot spice, and their stomachs begin to move within them. Finally Pilar stands up.

Fuck it, he says.

There is a man inside, and he lets the boys come in. On a stove, there is a skillet cooking. It has a mixture of cornbread, beans, and onions. The seasoning is ground ginger and hot sauce. The boys are given warm tortillas and they take scoops out of the skillet with them and eat.

They sit on a sofa, and the man sits on the floor before a walnut coffee table. He has a shawl that he keeps around his shoulders. The man doesn't seem to want to talk, or the boys think maybe he has a hard time speaking. There is a television on the floor, but it has no cord, and if it did, there would be nothing to plug it into. Facile asks the man how to find the town ahead.

This is where I live, replies the man.

Pilar and Facile aren't sure what to say. They finish their meal, and then they sit silently together in the dark. After a while, the man gets up and leaves the house. They hear him walk around out back, and then the motor of a generator struggles into life. Suddenly, a little light bulb overhead flickers on.

I don't like to be bothered, says the man, coming back inside.

They begin to stand up to leave, but the man tells them they can stay. He sets out pallets of blankets for them to sleep on, and, lying on the floor, Pilar and Facile talk about Hector.

How long before he finds us? says Facile.

Not long.

That son of a bitch. Where should we go?

I don't know.

In the morning, they drink cold coffee and have eggs. The man is more friendly towards them, and he tells them how to find the town ahead. As they take the footpath back into the forest brush, the goat follows them for a distance, and then disappears.

Chapter 6

Randy crosses the Guatemalan border at the little border station. He shows his passport and then rides through. He is in love with his new motorcycle. It pulls through the mountains with ease. On the hillsides, he rides past fields of vegetables where stands of short corn cling to the shallow soil. And he passes, too, small plantations of leafy banana and cacao trees. In the basin, at the bottom of the mountain, is the city, and it spreads its long arms across the valley, like a pale creature sunning itself.

He keeps to the west, and after a few days of riding, he comes to the coastline. As he rides, the spectre of twin volcanoes rise up sheer in the distance. Their brown caps are sharp above the forested hills. He rides into a little port town, the smell of the coast blowing salty and ripe. Alongside him, the Pacific rolls in gray barrels, topped with white foam.

He lingers for a while on the coast, loathe to leave the sunshine and the waves. He goes out in the afternoons and fishes for marlin. On a clear morning, at a little cafe, he sits in a wire mesh chair on the sunny patio. He drinks his coffee with a little milk. His motorcycle leans on its stand in the street.

After a while, a little scooter comes down the street, with two boys riding its seat. They park in front of the cafe, and sit down at the table across from him. He nods to them.

A woman comes out and asks the boys what they want.

We don't have any money, says Facile.

For a second, the waitress taps her foot, and then she goes back inside. They watch her go in, and then Randy calls to them across the patio.

I like your scooter, he says. I had one just like it when I lived in the Philippines.

I like yours better, says Pilar.

He buys them coffee and sandwiches, and they eat and enjoy the sunshine together. Seabirds scrabble across the stone around them, looking for scraps. After they eat, they get up and look over their machines, admiring the graceful steel in the sunlight.

You don't know where we could find some work around here, do you? says Facile.

There's a few boats at the port down the road, says Randy. They might need some extra hands.

The dock down at the beach is a small one, and Pilar and Facile find it easily. Only a few boats list atop the waves, tethered to the gray wood. They find a man lying in the hold of the first boat they come to. He has a hat covering his face, and the back of his head is resting in his laced fingers. The boat is a big one, with a berth below deck and a cabin above.

Hey, says Facile.

The man pushes his hat back.

Do you need any help?

Does it look like I need help?

Down the way is a smaller boat, open keeled, and there is a man preparing nets within it. He balances in the little skiff, laying the nets out in careful folds. The boys stand and watch him.

You need any help?

He pauses his work, and looks up at them.

Sure.

On the water, the boys cling tightly to the sides of the skiff, as it heaves like a rocking horse through the surf. The outboard motor smokes like a chimney behind them. Pilar shakes his head as the water sprays up into the boat, soaking them.

When the coastline disappears, the man turns off the motor, and the boat goes quiet. His name is Hiram. He is a little man, with teeth nubbed down to his gums, and a short laugh that rockets into a high pitch. He seems to laugh at awkward times, when things aren't funny.

He maneuvers nimbly around the boat, but the boys are clumsy as they pull on the nets, upsetting the skiff. The ocean is massive around them. The wind stirs the boat in a circle. Hiram throws out the nets, and the skeins pull through the water behind them as he trolls the motor.

After a while, the nets begin to draw heavily, their wires filled with little bait fish.

Okay, says Hiram. Pull them in.

By the end of the day, the hands of the boys are raw, and their backs and arms burn with fatigue. Hiram sits in the boat calmly. He watches them work, happy to have the ignorance of youth carrying the burden.

I sell the baitfish to the gringos, he says. They come down here to fish for marlin.

The boat is full of fish, and Pilar worries it might sink. There is no land anywhere close. Hiram goes back to the motor and hits the starter button, but nothing happens.

Uh oh, he says. I think we're out of gas.

The boys look at him, and he laughs his high laugh.

Just kidding.

He takes the boys home with him, and his wife makes them dinner. They live in a little shack, inland, close to the mountains. They eat boiled shrimp with cabbage and rice, served in a fresh tomato stew. The wife is suspicious of the boys, and she makes her doubts known. After the meal, Hiram tells them they are not welcome to stay the night.

I'm sorry, he says, laughing awkwardly. Ever since I cheated on her, my wife doesn't trust me. If you need a place to sleep, there is a shed just a little ways into the woods. It has my fishing tackle in it. You should be able to spread your pallets out on the floor.

They do, and they lie next to one another in the shed. They make room for the scooter inside, too.

What do you think? says Facile.

I'm not going back out in that damn boat, says Pilar.

Outside, the little tree frogs are as loud as sirens.

No. I guess not.

Chapter 7

Randy makes his way north along the Pacific coast. He has no itinerary. The motorcycle hums beneath him, long shocked and well sprung. He meanders along the back alleys of the coastal towns, waving at the children as he passes. The streets are narrow, cut into the blocks of tight houses and shaded with flowering trees.

The mountains rise up to the east, lush with green vegetation. He follows the highway up into the forests, where the howler monkeys hang in the canopy. The spanish moss drapes everything like an ancient beard. Walnut trees grow up next to the wild fruit, and tender succulents cling to the crevices in the limestone.

He stops along the roadside shoulder, and watches a hummingbird drink from a bright red orchid bloom. On the other side of the guard rail is a sinkhole, lined with lush grass and ferns. He walks along its edge, following its path as it snakes through the ground. Up from its depths, he can hear the trickle of groundwater.

He finds an opening large enough to fit through, and drops down into it. The water lightly splashes in its runnel of limestone. There is enough light to see the moss that furs the ground below him. For a while, he stares into the darkness, gaging how deep the cavern might go. He takes a loose rock and throws it, listening to its distant clatter. A few bats wing up past him.

He makes a camp in the hole, and sleeps well. Sometime in the night, there is a body next to him. Its claws scrabble on the rock, and in the water. He opens his eyes, and tries to look through the darkness, but sees nothing. A curious nose sniffs him through his blanket. He thinks it is some kind of dog, and it smells like wet hair and grease. He keeps still, and after a while, he doesn't hear it anymore.

In the morning, he climbs up out of the hole, and sees the world, bright and green. From the leaves of the trees, a wetness drips lightly. He squats beneath a tall sweet gum and takes a shit, and he admires the slender ficus ingrown to its trunk. On the seat of his motorcycle, there is a layer of dew, and he wipes it down before getting on.

The road winds along the high ridge, and as the tires take up the bumps and the divets, he and the motorcycle share a common spirit. In the afternoon, he rides down through a shallow plain, surrounded by a prairie of wide faced sunflowers and purple asters.

Over the next few days, as he travels further north, the mountains begin to ridge along lands of arid mesas. The lush grass turns short and dry, and the trees squat into dark shrubs. The birds, too, move like small darts through the air.

On a cool evening, he stops in a small town in northwest Mexico and finds a place to eat. He gets a bowl of potato soup with green onions and a skillet of sizzling beef. The cafe is small, and he sits in a booth beside a window with a cup of coffee. Outside, in the street, he sees two boys drive by on a lime green scooter. He recognizes them as the boys from the coast.

Randy thinks about the chances of his and the boys' paths crossing again, here in Mexico. Funny how that works, he thinks. A world that can hold eight billion people, and our paths crossing like that. He wonders where they might be headed, and where they are coming from.

And he thinks, too, about the forces that determine the paths of a person's life. He suddenly feels very small, and inadequate. At forty years old, he is discovering his own lack of control over his life, and of the swirling world around him. These are thoughts that occupy his mind, as he eats alone in the little cafe.

Chapter 8

Atop the high mountain in El Gueguecho, Esda finds work in the coffee fields. The morning mist wraps her like a scarf as she works. The cherries are bright red, scattered on the ground beneath the trees like beads. She gathers them in a bag strung on her shoulder, humming softly to herself.

Through the heavy mist, the sun is muted into something like moonlight. She leans down and takes a cherry in her fingers. It is smooth skinned and slightly oblong. She puts it in her teeth, and skins the flesh, and thinks about Pilar, and what he might be doing.

And among the lonely evenings, she finds a sweetheart. His name is Nerlan, and he works in the repair shop below her flat. She and Asa like to sit in the shop and watch him work. He moves among the guts of the washing machines like a butcher to a carcass. Replacing the electric motor of a washer, he strings the belt through the pulley, and the bucket of the machine spins like a carousel.

What do you think of that? says Nerlan, looking at Asa.

She spins a ratchet in her fingers and laughs. Her eyes are as big as buttons.

Within her mountain community, Esda is looked on as someone who knows something of the outside world. When she speaks at school meetings, or at the neighborhood football games, she is listened to. The community knows the dangers they face. The security forces hired by the dam company skulk around town like vipers. They are impossible to tell from the regular policemen, and even from the military.

And yet the town is a vibrant place, ancient and full of spirit. Music and singing erupt from the brightly painted houses like blooming flowers. Gatherings are held at the river, to remind the people of what the water means to them.

On a sunny day, Nerlan carries Asa on his shoulders as he wades into the current of the river. He follows a little sandbar that comes out of the woods. There are a few others at the river's edge, talking and fishing. Beneath the water, his toes are dark and furry. Asa laces her fingers around his forehead, and rides him like a jockey. He picks up speed, and the water splashes up around his legs.

Ayeee! Nerlan!

Esda rolls up her khakis and wades in with them. She thinks about her mother and father in this river. How it had given them life. How they had depended on it for their basic needs. As the water rolls across her ankles, she gets a feeling she cannot explain. Something that pulls her in a direction she cannot see. It is a pleasant feeling.

She gets invited to represent the Lenca people in Tegucigalpa at a public protest. The government has just held an election, one that many believe to be fraudulent. She and Nerlan sit at the dinner table to discuss it. He doesn't like it. He blows on his hot coffee in a concerned fashion.

They will murder you there, he says.

They are murdering us here, says Esda.

And so, on a dark morning, she gets in a car with a few others. They drive across the long mountains, the forested hills.

The dark trees lunge and swirl. She sleeps. When she wakes, the car is stopped. They are still on the road, but there are tires stacked in a wall across the highway. A few people stand before them. The car turns around, and goes another way.

The people are trying to keep the military out of the city, says the driver.

As they come into Tegucigalpa, passing through the narrow neighborhoods, Esda thinks about the years past when she brought Pilar down from the mountains. He had been sick from the mercury in the river water. He was yellowish and undersized. She wonders where he might be right now. And her heart hurts.

The city is in turmoil. In the business district, the people pack the streets. They push against the barricades built by the police. They shout into the glass windowed cafes, where the businessmen and politicians strike deals. They cry out about education, about the privatization of healthcare. They want the world to know that the president's brother is a known drug runner.

And around them, lining the roofs, are the policemen, the military, and the private security forces. They wear American tactical gear. They carry American rifles with American bullets. Behind one of the masks, standing in a row of masks that look just like his, is Hector. He is waiting, patiently.

Esda and her group move through the crowd. She is escorted to a little podium, where the microphone has to be lowered for her to speak into it. The top of her head can just be seen over the podium. She doesn't know if anyone can hear her. She shakes violently.

She talks about the Lenca people and mother earth. She says they can no longer afford to be hostages in the race to industrialize her homeland. It's time for our people to rise up and take back our role as caretakers and stewards of the land, she says.

She walks away from the podium, and stands on the stage. She can hardly hear or see the people around her. She can't make out what the other speakers say. As the minutes pass by, she becomes keenly aware of the policemen, their masks and bulletproof vests. It is a sickening feeling. She is filled only with the desire to return home.

And when she does make it home, she has never felt so happy to hold Asa in her arms. The sickness falls away, and there is a peace in her little flat. When Nerlan comes over, he holds her tightly, and kisses her hair.

I'm proud of you, he says.

Chapter 9

When the weather begins to turn cool, Pilar and Facile come to the Sonoran desert. They ride over long stretches of highway, the dusty hills filled with gray desert scrub and dry grass. A few sheer rocks rise up and ridge the distance.

The long barrels of gasoline trucks pass by them, blowing the little scooter across the asphalt. They cross a high canyon, in the bottom of which a green snake of water flows. Along its edges, a few stands of willow and elm grow up, carpeted with bright green grass. Further on, they can see where the water is piped out to the plain, and long fields of lettuce shade the ground green.

They watch the workers in the fields, their slender backs bent to the lettuce. They are shrouded in mist. The boys follow the highway up out of the canyon and back into the hills. The road begins to wind up around the ridged land. The sharp backs of the hills are perforated with cactus and prickly pear, and dense thickets of thorn scrub.

They ride all day and come to a little desert town in the evening. There are a few old structures of stone along the road, with wrought iron gates and flat roofs. They pass alongside a market with stands of squash and corn and green melons, and then they park in the square. In a little cafe, they eat burnt ends with beans and rice and drink horchata. A pretty waitress serves them, and they watch her with goggle eyes.

You're going north, aren't you? she says.

They nod in agreement.

You're going to die in the desert.

The comment sours them. That night, they sleep outside, and let the sky shine above them. The desert dogs yip somewhere out there.

What should we do when we cross the border? says Facile.

Probably find girlfriends.

Ya. Probably.

Across the next few days, the towns become further apart along the highway. The ridges spike up higher, and they find themselves looking out over a long land of bone like rises and depressions. They watch a thunderstorm brew somewhere south on the horizon.

Atop a ridge, surrounded by a forest of blue oak scrub, the piston in the little scooter seizes. They try to kick it over, but it's locked in the cylinder.

It's probably all the dust, says Facile.

What, are you a fucking mechanic now?

I don't know.

You're probably right.

The task of crossing the desert now is a daunting one. They walk, and they walk for a long time. They eat no food and they drink no water and they sleep in bowls of igneous rock where tender succulents throw out trumpet blooms.

This was a mistake, says Facile.

Further north, the land irons out before them into a pan of brown dust and gray thorn scrub. The road now is little more than a clearing through the brush. They stagger until they can walk no more, and then they sit beneath a tall yucca tree.

Jesus Christ, says Pilar.

Leaning against the base of the tree, they watch a desert tortoise scrabble past. It has a carved shell and its sharp claws dig in the rock and dirt. They watch its scrawny legs propel its bulk across the rock. After a while, they hear the whine of a motor across the desert emptiness. And then they see a rider on a motorcycle.

Randy stops before them, and shuts off his bike. He takes off his helmet.

You ok? he says.

We could use a ride, says Facile.

They squeeze together on the bike, and Randy manages the awkward weight as he maneuvers across the desert. The big barrel cactuses grow up around them, making shapes like awkward crosses. After so long, Randy notices a shadow on the ground following his bike, and he looks up to see a drone pasted against the sky like a distant gnat. And then not long after that, three Border Patrol agents on four wheelers intercept them.

The agents are marked in tactical gear and helmets, and Randy stops the bike and turns it off. He pulls his helmet from his head and waits. As the agents approach, guns drawn, the boys get nervous.

Stay calm, says Randy.

So they do.

Chapter 10

With their murder charges back in Honduras, Pilar and Facile are deported before they get access to a phone call. They fly back down to Tegucigalpa, and have a very public trial. Pilar and Facile, handcuffed, pose for photographs with masked policemen. Hector is among them. The dam company pays for the prosecution, and the judge rails in his seat against the dangers of wayward youth. The American ambassador even makes an appearance, promising more support for the Honduran security forces.

Over the next few weeks, Pilar is transferred between different units in the prison, from general population, to isolation, and back again. At one point, they put him in a cage no larger than a dog kennel. So when the guard comes in and tells him he has a visitor, he feels a surge of excitement.

But he is quickly disappointed when he walks into the room and sees Hector sitting at the table. He sits down, and Hector throws a pack of cigarettes onto the tabletop. Pilar looks at the guard, and then he takes one, and they smoke together.

I wanted to come and apologize, says Hector. It was nothing personal. I like you. You and Facile both. I'm just like you. I just got lucky. You got unlucky.

Well, says Pilar.

Hector wears an impeccable uniform. His blue shirt, tucked into his pants, displays his rank and insignia. He waves the guard out of the room, and leans forward.

I mean that, he says. Just because I'm in this uniform, doesn't make me any better than you. I grew up in the same neighborhoods you did, remember.

He leans back in his chair.

I heard you tried to go to America.

Ya, we did.

Did you know I've been there? We went up there for officer training. It was a hoot. Everything was so fucking official. They made us feel important, you know? Like we weren't just boys from Tegucigalpa.

For a moment, Hector's face grows serious as he leans over the table.

But I learned a lesson, then, he says. That we are just boys from the barrio, me and you. That's the thing. We've got no pull, one way or another. You got caught up in a system Pilar, one that was designed without us in mind. We have no place in it. And I got to see a little bit of that system, in America. Just a piece of it, but I saw it. I got to see who really pulls the strings down here. And when I saw it, Pilar, it scared me.

The little visitor room is quiet, with Hector and Pilar the only occupants. There is a window in the upper corner of the wall that sheds a little daylight onto the men.

I knew it could have been me in this cell, says Hector, just as easy as you. So I made a decision. What else can we do, Pilar? This world was not made for boys from Tegucigalpa. I hope you won't judge me.

Pilar leans back and laughs, a heavy gout of smoke chugging from his blowhole. He scratches his hair, out of which the dandruff falls like snow. For the first time in his life, he feels like an adult, trying to balance the crushing burden of existence.

I don't blame you, he says. I probably would have made the same decision.

If you need any help in here, let me know, says Hector.

Thanks, but I think I've had enough of your help.

Not long after that, Pilar is taken from his cell again, and told he has another visitor. He expects to see Hector once again, asking him to do some job in the lock up. But when he sees Esda sitting at the table, his heart bursts.

I've been bamboozled, mama, he says.

I know, Pilar. I'm sorry.

They sit across the table from one another, and Esda takes his hand. Pilar's facial structure has changed since she last saw him. His cheek bones have broadened, and his nose is bigger. His eyes seem like stamps in his face.

They're going to murder me in here, he says.

No they're not, says Esda. Don't say that. I want you to know that I am here Pilar. All of us are. Nerlan, Asa, all of our people. We are witnesses to your experience. And we are going to work outside of here, Pilar, so you must work inside.

Even in this dark place, Pilar, there is life. It is in you, and it is in the people around you. It is in the guard sitting at the end of this table. So don't shut down, and don't shut it out. Help the people around you. If you see someone suffering, help them. And, God willing, one day we will tear down these walls that keep us apart.

They seperate, and Pilar walks the long hallway back to the prison. He finds Facile sitting in the common area, on the bleachers. Pilar sits next to him.

Did you tell her it was my fault? says Facile.

Yes I did.

And what did she say?

She said we need to learn to help people.

They look around the room, where other men sit and talk. They are old and young together, and fits of laughter peal across the room.

Ya, says Facile. But who's gonna help us?

Chapter 11

Back in Tucson, Randy goes back to work. He works in a corporate office building, the glass of which reflects the high desert sun. He has a corner office, and the windows look out on the street below. He is watching the empty desert sky when his boss comes in.

Hey Ron, he says.

Good to see you, Randy.

They embrace, and then sit across from one another at Randy's desk. The plans for the dam are laid out, and the sunlight comes through the window and illuminates them.

What do you think? says Ron.

The plans are all good. They're fine, says Randy.

You went over everything?

Ya, I did.

Randy pauses, and then says, I had a little trouble coming across the border. I picked up a couple boys on my motorcycle in the desert. Now they tell me they want to charge me with smuggling.

They're assholes down at the border, says Ron. You can't even leave the country now without it being a pain in the ass. We support you one hundred percent, Randy. Let us know whatever legal help you need.

Randy is still watching out the window. He changes the subject.

What do you know about the dam company down there?

In Honduras?

Ya.

Nothing. Why?

I think they might be doing some shady things down there. I met a lawyer while I was in El Gueguecho. He represented the people who live on the land where the dam company wants to do the project. I think they're called Lenca. He was murdered while I was down there.

The lawyer?

Ya.

Jesus.

Ron expects Randy to go on, but he doesn't.

What do you think we should do? says Ron.

I don't know. Do you think we should do business with people like that?

I don't make those decisions, and neither do you.

Someone does.

We're just engineers, Randy.

Ron gets up to leave.

I just think it's wrong to contract with businesses like that, says Randy.

I'll put in a complaint with the board, Randy. I'll make sure your concerns are known.

Later on, in his little house, Randy lies on his bed with one foot on the floor. He feels as though the world might be upside down, and he might slip off the mattress at any time. He tries to watch the television, but can't seem to get interested. His dog sleeps at the foot of the bed. He thinks about calling his ex-wife, and talking to his son. He thinks about the forest and the mountain and the river. He thinks about Pilar and Facile, and he wishes he could see them again. He knows that these feelings will pass, but he avoids sleep, to hold on to them a while longer.

PART 3: SOUTHWEST ASIA

Chapter 1

In Yemen, Byron's hotel is on the port of Aden, and he spends his time watching the boats come and go. The sea port is a thoroughfare of cargo ships, crude oil tankers, and fishing boats. Around the giant hulls of cargo ships, the little fishing skiffs buzz like insects. He brings a chair out onto his balcony and watches them.

And he eats in the little restaurants along the street. He eats beef tibs and spicy lentils with a bread that reminds him of pancakes. He drinks ginger root beer with it. Outside, the traffic in the street is constant. A conglomeration of white taxi vans and Chinese motorcycles that seem to stream on repeat ceaselessly.

Later on, he finds the old markets, and traverses the ancient stone corridors. The stalls are laden with fabric and spices, silk and cotton and cardamom and turmeric. The lips of the burlap sacks are rolled down to reveal the fine red and green and yellow powders. And the crates of wheat and barley flour are stacked side by side with the plantains and yams and onions.

As he roams the streets, he feels restless. He wants something to happen, but isn't sure what. He has been in a hundred foreign cities, and this one doesn't feel particularly different. He finds a little cafe, where a few men sit at the tables and talk. They glance at him, and then don't look at him again.

In the morning, he meets with his driver, Askar, and they ride together through the city. They ride in a Toyota FJ cruiser, and Byron appreciates the leather interior. He tells Askar a little bit about himself, and where he would like to go, and then they don't say much. Byron watches the streets pass by out the window.

At the edge of the city, a ridge of sheer rock rises like the spiky back of some extinct lizard. It's crescent ridge holds back the city from the coastal plains. They cross the high rock, following a road that switchbacks down the steep face of the mountain. A few houses cling to the sides of the sharp rock. They are square concrete structures with flat roofs, and they seem to crop up from the rock itself. The terraced ridges around them are dotted with fruit trees and vegetable gardens. Stone corrals, holding goats and sheep, tilt along the hillsides.

After they cross the mountains, the plains stretch out before them, divided into long fields of grain, sorghum and barley. Byron watches a few women in headscarves bend to the barley, cradling the sheaves in their arms. Askar drives Byron all day across the plain, travelling northward. In the afternoon, they begin to come to the checkpoints.

There are men standing along the road, and the SUV slows down as they approach. The men wear corduroy vests over their white tunics, with sandals. Askar rolls down the window, and talks to the men. They look at Byron, and he doesn't say anything.

They continue on, stopping for the night in a little town at the foot of another mountain range. The lights of the houses glow up in the shadow of the dark ridge behind them. Against the starlight, the mountains are sheer and jagged and opaque. The streets are quiet, without much traffic. They pass through a neighborhood of houses, low structures of brick, fenced about with iron and concrete.

At the outskirts of the town, up in the foothills, they stop at a little compound. It has a few lights hung atop tall light poles. They shine down on the main building, with a few out buildings around it. Fig trees and acacia scrub hedge the concrete. They pass through the gates, and a few men come out to meet them. A few dogs do, too.

After a brief conversation, Byron and Askar go inside and sit on sofas around a low table. There is a hookah, and the men sit and smoke. The fragrant embers fill the room. After a while, plates of food are brought in, fried flat bread with lamb meat cooked in a broth of garlic and onion. They drink coffee, too. Some of the men chew qat, and as Byron puts the leaves in his mouth, they laugh as he grimaces at the texture.

Later in the night, Byron and Askar sleep on cots in an outbuilding, ensconced among garden tools and implements. Just a little light comes through the window, into the dark shed.

How was your trip into Aden? says Askar.

It was good, says Byron.

Did you come through Jedda?

Yes, I did.

Askar and Byron are about the same age, and probably have much in common. Both are professionals, trying to navigate a fractious world. They are only now beginning to feel comfortable around one another. They listen to the dark outside.

Are you married? says Askar.

No. Are you?

No.

They are quiet for a minute, and then Askar asks him why he isn't married.

I don't know, says Byron. I guess because I haven't wanted to. Why aren't you married?

I am saving my money. I have a girlfriend in Sana'a. Her name is Naimi.

And then Askar asks him if he has been with a woman. Byron laughs.

Yes, I have.

Byron listens to a cricket squeak somewhere in the shed, and then he hears Askar's sleepy breathing. He tries to sleep, but he feels restless. It could be the qat, or the coffee. He feels nervous, as if there might be someone outside the shed. He knows this isn't true.

Byron's anxiety has been flaring up lately, affecting his work at the State Department. The panic attacks usually hit right before the trips abroad. It is something deeply subconscious, something he cannot explain. It begins with an elevated heartbeat, and moves into his tense muscles, and then goes into a crippling feeling of paralysis. As if he is completely unable to function at any level.

He has tried a few different medications, with little success. These are the things he thinks about as he lies on his cot, in the quiet dark shed. After a while, he falls asleep.

Chapter 2

Naimi works in a hotel in Sana'a, splitting shifts between the front desk and the cleaning staff. She makes good money, plenty to feed herself with and pay the rent for her little apartment, and send money back to her mother. She came here from Somaliland, looking for work. She had been living with her mother, with no way to support herself.

Here, in Sana'a, the rich Saudis and Emaratis come to do business, staying in the lavish hotels in the business district. Naimi's long wrap sweeps across the ornate tile as she works the front desk. She passes keys, and smiles widely. Sometimes, a cash tip is passed across the counter to her.

On a chilly morning, colder than usual, she wakes up sick. She stands over the sink, vomiting. She wipes her lips, and splashes her face with water. The acid burns her throat, and leaves a sour taste in her mouth. Her tongue clings to her teeth. She tries to call the hotel, but her phone doesn't work. She tries to call Askar in Aden but gets nothing.

She listens outside. It is very quiet. Her neighbors, too, are quiet. Usually, their voices and the cries of children pierce the paper thin walls. She goes to the window, and looks down into the street. There is nothing moving. She steps out onto the balcony, a little alcove of concrete. Clotheslines criss cross from balcony to balcony, draped with bright fabric. They flutter in the sunlight. Across the city, steel water tanks stand atop the flat concrete roofs.

The first blast knocks Naimi from her feet, and she leans against the concrete wall. Above the dense neighborhood, a column of smoke rises. She makes it back inside as the shells begin to fall like rain. The concussions shake her little apartment. She begins to panic, not sure what to do. For a long time, she just stands in the middle of her room, listening to the blasts, one after the other, expecting them to end. But they don't.

She goes downstairs, to the woman's apartment below her.

What is it? says Naimi.

I don't know, says the woman.

They sit together at a table and drink tea. The woman's name is Abeedah, and she is the same age as Naimi's mother. She lives with her son and his wife, but they are not at the apartment. The concussions from the blasts seem to take on a physical aspect in the little room, taking the place of conversation between the two women.

Twilight finds the two women still sitting on the floor, at the low table. Abeedah rises, and lights a candle. Its fragile flame shakes among the falling dust and debris from the concussions. There is no electricity. Naimi reclines on a pillow, against the couch, and listens to the blasts. It seems they will never end.

She wakes up sometime in the night, and realizes the blasts have stopped. The candle has burned down its long stem, and the flame gutters lightly in a pool of wax. Abeedah is still sitting upright, but seems to be asleep. Naimi falls asleep again, and when she wakes up, this time, there is daylight leaking in at the window.

Now, the artillery blasts have been replaced with the shouts of men. They call out to one another in the streets. And then the gunfire begins. It claps around the neighborhood like applause for an evil sideshow. At one point, the two women think they hear the bullets shattering a window and crossing the apartment next to them.

After a few hours of this, they start upright when there is a knocking on Abeedah's door. Slowly, Abeedah rises and opens it. A man comes in and looks around the room. He looks at Naimi, and then at Abeedah. He wears a white tunic with a brown vest, and carries a rifle. He walks into the adjoining room, and looks around. Then he comes back out, and leaves.

The fighting lasts for three days, and neither Abeedah nor Naimi leave the apartment. They eat rice and canned tomatoes, and sleep on the floor. When Naimi goes to the sink to vomit, Abeedah watches her. She brings her a wet washcloth and wipes her face and mouth with it.

Well, says Abeedah. At least there is something good among all this sadness.

Eventually, the fighting dies down, and after a day of silence, Naimi goes outside and walks down the street. The cars are overturned, and burned out. Fallen concrete is scattered around the street. Windows are broken, and wrought iron and rebar are mangled.

She walks past a collapsed building, where a group is searching the ruins. There is a general wailing in the air, amidst the pauses of silence. For a moment, Naimi thinks about the people underneath the slabs of concrete, and then she forces the thought out of her mind. She keeps walking.

At the little market on the corner, she finds the front door open, but there is no one inside. The shelves are mostly empty. She finds a few bottles of water, a can of dates, a can of peas, and some bread.

For a few days, the city is quiet, and then the aerial bombardment begins. These explosions are less frequent, but much larger. When they occur, they bring down the buildings, jarring the very bones of the city. The nebulous steel and concrete that weaves the web of Naimi's world feels as if it is coming apart.

A few fighters come back into their building, and hide out in Naimi's apartment. Naimi and Abeedah listen to their sporadic firing above them.

You must leave the city, says Abeedah, after two weeks with no electricity and little food.

What about you? says Naimi.

I am just an old woman. If they kill me, shame on them.

Abeedah finds a ride out of the city for Naimi, and Naimi packs a bag with water and canned food and clothes and toiletries. She feels a little uncertain when she meets her carrier. He is a boy, no more than fourteen, spraddled on a long shocked motorcycle. His feet have trouble reaching the ground, and his toes stretch out from his sandals. When he tries to back up, his foot slips, and the bike falls over in front of Naimi.

Abeedah puts her hand on Naimi's back.

His name is Aflaw, she says. He will take you safely to Aden where you can find Askar.

Naimi gathers her wrap around her, and helps Aflaw pick up the bike. She steps onto the back seat, and Aflaw adjusts with her weight. Soon, they are flitting lightly through the streets, leaning easily around stalled traffic and ruined roads. Naimi feels a slight thrill as the machine picks up speed, carrying her like a lean horse. Her garments flag around her as she holds tightly to the rear handholds, and her travel bag hangs behind her. She hopes Askar is in Aden.

Chapter 3

Byron and Askar drive further into the mountains, the SUV's transmission whining up the steep grades. The road winds around the rock that shoves upwards in sharp protrusions from the earth. All up the mountainsides, the soil is cut into stepped terraces that are cultivated with coffee and quat and fruit shrubs. Byron lays his chin in his hand and watches the landscape pass.

Around midday, they park atop a summit and look down into the long valley, in the depths of which a pale town lies sunning itself. Around it, the peaks of the ridges fold up and cascade into one another. They eat lunch in the town and then continue on, driving further into the folds of the ridges.

They drive through a light rain shower, the mist of which hangs in the peaks like hair. The rain water funnels down the rocky culverts around the road, and Byron watches the windshield wipers sweep the droplets from the glass. They pass across an old stone bridge, the narrowness of which hardly allows the big SUV to pass over it. Looking over the parapet, Byron can see down into the deep ravine, across which the high stone arches. A tail of water trickles below.

In the afternoon, Askar parks along a high escarpment, where the concrete breaks up and trails off into a narrow pathway.

We'll have to walk from here, he says.

Byron gets out of the car and looks around. A cold wind blows across the mountain. It whistles in the branches of the juniper scrub and shakes the leaves of the carob trees. He feels very alone. They walk all day through the mountains, following footholds that cling to the narrow rockface. The world falls away below them into blue and gray depths.

Byron wears a backpack, and he stops periodically to drink water. They pass compounds in the high mountains, houses made from rocks stacked in precarious yet perfect walls. For a while, they walk with a boy taking his sheep to the river. The big animals shamble along a gravel swale that slopes gently to the water. The boy tells Askar about the sheep, how he doesn't like them.

They knocked my sister over, and butted her in the head, he says. Gave her a concussion. I found her wandering around the orchard, crying. I won't hesitate to shoot one of them.

He flips up his shirt, and shows them the pistol tucked into his pants. Askar laughs and claps him on the back.

What did he say? asks Byron.

He says he will shoot the sheep if they do anything stupid.

When it becomes dark, and Byron is finding it difficult to follow Askar's dark figure against the mountain, they see the lights of a little village. They are warm and flickering on the mountainside. Byron is exhausted and hungry, and doesn't pay much attention to his surroundings. They follow the road that switchbacks down into the community, and then they wind through the alleyways of stone houses and a few shops.

Askar leads him into a little house where he is given a plate of sauteed chicken with eggs and fried plantains and coffee to drink. He eats, and immediately feels better, leaning back in the chair in which he sits. It is a wooden chair with a tight straw weft, and he feels as if he could fall asleep instantly.

But when he is taken to his bed, he nods off and then wakes up again. This happens several times. Just as he falls asleep, his body shakes and his pulse rises. He realizes this is the anxiety, and he goes through his cognitive behavioral therapy to relax himself. He tells himself it is better to lie awake and rest, than walk around and fret all night. So that is what he does. It is a long night, and when he hears people stirring about the house in the morning, he feels as tired as he felt the night before.

He meets with a man in the afternoon, at a little shop in the village. There are a few other men with him, and Byron and Askar sit around a low table with them. They eat together, and then a hookah is brought in, and they smoke and listen to music. A block of frankincense resin lies smouldering on a burner, and fills the room with its heavy fragrance.

After a while, when they are full and sleepy, Byron takes a few papers from his backpack and sets them onto the table. No one seems to notice them, and after a few minutes pass, Byron slides them towards Hassan. He is an older man, and the wrinkles in his face trail down into his beard. The fabric of his suit coat is worn thin and the colors of his tunic beneath are sun bleached.

He takes a moment to look through the papers and then he sets them down. The other men around him are quiet now. Askar and Byron watch him.

Why are you here? he says.

Askar tells Byron what he said, and then Byron tells him that he is a representative of the State Department of the United States Government.

And what would you like from us?

We would like to enter into a contract with you, and provide you the means with which to defend yourselves.

Defend ourselves from whom?

From terrorists, and from those who would destroy your country.

And how do you know we are not the terrorists?

Because we have careful processes in place, to ensure our weapons end up in the hands of those with only the best interests in mind.

With your interests, in mind, you mean.

Askar goes to translate this, but Hassan waves him off. He points to another man at the table, and this man produces a blackened piece of shrapnel. He speaks English to Byron.

Do you know what this is?

No. I don't.

It's the fragment of a missile that struck my granddaughter's wedding party. Look at it.

He slides it across the table to Byron, and Byron takes it up in his hands. It is heavy steel and smells of burnt carbon. On the bottom, along the edge, is a Lockheed Martin serial number.

I don't know anything about this, says Byron.

Of course you don't, says the man. No one does. That's the problem. You come here, and speak in terms of good and bad, right and wrong. My family has been in these mountains for hundreds of years, and we have watched the empires come and go. And yours, too, will pass. We will survive. We don't want what you bring. You bring death and suffering. You arm everyone, all sides, and then watch the destruction.

The music still plays in the background, and the men lean back and smoke again. Byron takes the papers and puts them into his backpack. They sit for a little while longer, and then Byron and Askar thank them for the food, and leave.

They spend the night in the little village, and then, the next day, they drive back through the mountains. In the SUV, Askar asks Byron where he is from.

In America?

Yes.

Texas.

You're family, too?

Yes.

What about before?

Before what?

America.

You mean in Africa?

Yes.

Byron laughs.

I have no idea. That was a long time ago.

They ride in silence for a long time, and then Askar asks Byron if he has ever been to Africa.

Yes, I have. Have you?

No, but my girlfriend is from Somalia. Her name is Naimi.

Somalia is where I'm going to next, says Byron.

I'm sorry your deal did not work out.

That's okay. Thank you for your assistance. I appreciate it very much.

In the Toyota, Byron is able to sleep, and the soft rumble of the tires give him a deep, dreamless slumber. When he wakes, it is pitch dark, and the headlights of the SUV cut a rough yellow hole from the blackness. In the hole is a road, and nothing else.

Chapter 4

Aflaw and Naimi make it out of the city, and ride south through the mountains. They stop at several checkpoints, and Naimi pays cash to get herself and Aflaw through them. She is thankful she had money saved in her apartment. She also passes cash to Aflaw for gas, and buys him treats in the little shops at which they stop. They suck on candy as they ride.

Deeper in the mountains, the road climbs the tall peaks, and narrows in places down to a thin trail of gravel. At times, Aflaw maneuvers the bike around loose stone and rock, mere feet from a sheer precipice. Naimi's knuckles whiten around her handholds. As they navigate the sheep paths, she wonders why Aflaw left the highway, but then she reminds herself that Abeedah arranged the ride, and that she trusts her.

They spend the night in a little compound in the mountains, the house of which sits atop a rocky ledge. Aflaw and Naimi have a creamy soup of mushrooms and onions and visit with the family in the common area. There are a few women and children, and Hassan sits in a mahogany chair in the corner, smoking a pipe.

So they have taken Sana'a, he says.

Yes, says Naimi. The fighting is terrible.

They will blockade the ports now, and starve us out.

Before they go to bed, Naimi praises Aflaw's riding ability.

He brought us here without a single scratch, she says.

I've been riding motorcycles since I was three years old, says Aflaw. My father would strap me to his back and take me on rides. I have a picture of me and him, on a motorcycle, just like the one I have now, but older.

In the morning, they take their leave, and ride further south through the mountains. They cross an old stone bridge that arches over a high ravine. As they pass across it, Naimi wonders at how the stone can cling to the sheer rock, and how it may have been built. It reminds her of something out of a childhood fable.

The bike gains speed as the road widens out, the paved cement taking the place of the worn stone. Naimi begins to like the motorcycle, the feeling of its smooth acceleration, and she daydreams about her and Askar riding one together. She imagines her pregnant stomach pressed against his back. It makes her smile.

Around midday, the sharp ridges of the mountains pass behind them, and the flatlands of the coastal plains spread before them. The bike seems to eat the land in giant leaps, and Naimi feels as if she were flying.

By nightfall, they are in Aden, and at a small cafe, Naimi finds a place to charge her phone. She watches the bars rise, and then she calls Askar.

I'm in Aden, she says. I paid a carrier to bring me here.

Are you okay? says Askar.

Yes. But I'm pregnant.

Aflaw covers his ears as Naimi talks on the phone. He takes her to Askar's hotel, and when they get there, Naimi gives Aflaw a hug, and Askar gives him even more cash.

Thank you so much, says Naimi. I owe you my life.

Aflaw blushes, and rides off as quickly as he can, flush with cash. He feels big, alone in the port city with his motorcycle.

Like he could ride out onto the ocean, and cross the Gulf of Aden on it. Like he could go anywhere in the world.

He stops and eats at a restaurant, and the server eyes him with a curious glance.

You here by yourself? says the server.

They're bombing Sana'a, says Aflaw, with a gravity that belies his age.

He eats, and then rides down to the port, where the big ships linger in the dark. Along a sandy strand is a line of fishing skiffs that totter on the tide. They glitter with tackle in the moonlight. He wades into the water, and watches the jellyfish float past. They let the tide take them wherever it may.

Chapter 5

Byron rides in a boat with Askar and Naimi across the Gulf of Aden, to Somalia. The boat is crowded, filled with migrants who once came looking for work, now fleeing back the same way they came. The vessel on which they ride is a double decked fishing boat, converted now to haul migrants, and it lists heavily under the weight of the passengers.

The trip takes two days. Byron and Askar play cards on the outer deck, in the sunshine. The sea is expansive around the boat, and the air blusters up from the spumy water. A few sea birds roost in the tackle, preening their gray and white feathers.

Naimi sits with another passenger, talking about Somalia. Askar has a pack of cigarettes, and passes them around to others on the boat. The people are tired and anxious. They eat the canned food they brought with them, and everyone uses the same toilet, flushed into the ocean.

In the evening of the second day, they come into Berbera. The fishing boat gets led in by a tug into the port, around the big container ships that float like giants in the water. The big cranes work in the shipyard, their long necks lifting containers from the ships onto the cement loading docks. The passengers disembark from the boat, and then they are funneled into the customs offices. Byron helps Askar and Naimi find the refugee assistance shelter, and then he tells them goodbye. He wishes them luck with their pregnancy.

In the city, he finds a bus up to Djibouti, and sleeps most of the way. Sometime in the morning, he wakes up, and the bus is stopped on the side of the road. He isn't sure why. He looks out the window, and sees the sun hanging above the arid land like a lizard's eye. The short scrub greens the sand around the bus. He sees a few people out there, squatting, their bare asses protruding like mangoes.

The bus goes on, and after a few more hours, it comes into Djibouti City. The streets are busy, and Byron watches the traffic swirl around the bus. The restaurants and markets are clogged with people, and as the bus stops in a busy square, Byron gets his bag and gets off.

The sun is now high and glares off the brightly painted concrete around him. The noise of the street congestion mixes with the chatter of the crowded market. Flocks of sparrows and starlings scatter around the sidewalks and under the awnings. Byron gets a roasted lamb kebab and drinks a coffee, and then gets a taxi to Camp Lemonnier.

The gates of the base are open, and Byron walks up to the guard shack and shows his I.D. The man in the booth looks at it, and then gives it back to him. The sidewalks and lawns inside the base are hedged with bean shrubs and well manicured with dry grass. Byron takes note of the clean concrete and the swept streets.

The administration buildings rise up behind the lawns in sparkling brick and glittering windows. He walks around a fountain that streams water quietly, and then he enters the State Department building. After he submits his paperwork, and makes a few phone calls, he walks down to the base hotel and gets a room.

Before he goes back to the States, he spends a few days on the coast, watching the Red Sea roll onto the beach. He sits in a lounge chair with his ankles crossed, holding a cold drink in a cool glass. A few palms spring up in the sand around him, along with pink flowers on green vines. The water is blue and rolls in white caps onto the brown sand. Off in the far distance is a light sky.

He thinks about Yemen, out there across the water. He can't see it, but he knows it's there. An idea pops into his mind, and it makes his stomach turn. He knows the weapons he pushes in Yemen have no accountability, and that they are designed that way. And he has the paperwork to prove it.

He pushes the idea from his mind, and vows not to think about it until he returns to the States. He measures his breathing, and matches the rhythm of the rolling tide. A peaceful feeling comes over him. The evening sun on the water finds him asleep in his chair, with no thought of the future, or what it might hold.

Chapter 6

In Maryland, Byron goes back to work at his office. The building is a nondescript brick structure in the suburbs of D.C., and Byron spends most of his time there when he isn't overseas. His days are filled with paperwork and briefings, and he spends hours giving the same reports to different people in different ways.

He broods on his idea about the weapons now that he is back in the States, and it begins to consume more and more of his thoughts. His anxiety about it, too, grows. On a sweltering day in August, when the war in Yemen has reached a fever pitch, Byron meets with a journalist in an open park. The grass around them has yellowed from the heat, and the bench on which they sit is ensconced among the shade of a broad leafed maple.

Byron tugs at the tie around his neck.

Thank you for coming, he says.

He tells the journalist about Yemen, about the starvation, the cholera, the deaths of thousands of children.

I am a part of that process, he says. I am personally accountable. So is my boss, and his boss, and his boss, and his boss. But they don't want to acknowledge it. I have paperwork tracing these weapons, and they've been used to bomb hospitals, schools, water supplies, and food warehouses. These are American weapons used to commit war crimes.

Byron looks out on an expansive lawn, in the middle distance of which is a pond ringed with blue spruce and green pines. The journalist beside him is named Angela, and she wipes a bit of sweat from the back of her neck, and then looks over at him.

You know the risks, right? she says. I can protect my sources, but they will come after you.

Byron tries to think about it, but his thoughts seem to melt in the sweltering heat, and won't go anywhere. He has trouble comprehending her words.

Whatever you do, she says, don't talk to the feds. Ever.

A few weeks after the article is published, the FBI knocks on the door of his apartment. He lives in a swanky complex, with an open floored studio and fully walled windows that face the setting sun. The two agents are tall men in polo shirts and khakis, and they tell him they just want to talk. He tells them he has nothing to say.

So they get a warrant, and raid his apartment. They take his laptop and his phone, his briefcase and filing cabinet. They raid his office in the State Department building, too. His Top Secret clearance is stripped, and he can no longer go to work. He gets a lawyer, and waits.

The waiting is the hardest part. A full year passes from the time he is charged with mishandling classified materials to his trial date. He can't work, and he maxes out his credit cards on lawyer fees. His anxiety spirals out of control, and he stays in Texas with his parents. They provide him with a secure backstop, keeping him from falling into the caverns of hopelessness.

On a late night, unable to sleep, Byron walks the floor of his parent's house, and his father comes out to sit with him. His father is a big man, and fills the easy chair in his pajamas and slippers. His name is Eldridge. He rocks the chair in the living room gently, back and forth, waiting for his son to speak. He does.

I remember when I was just a junior officer in the Navy, says Byron, still pacing the floor. We were all out at a restaurant, eating. We weren't in our uniforms or anything, but you could tell we were all military. We all had the buzz cuts and bare faces. And these two women come up and start talking to us at our table, asking us if we're from the base, and asking us about what we do in the military.

They're these two older black ladies, and they're talking with us and joking around and having a good time. So we invite them to sit down at our table, and they do, and we're just talking, like we were. And then one of the ladies turns to me, and looks me dead in the eye, and asks me if I'm this crew's mascot. Because I'm the only black guy at this table, and she thinks I must be some kind of house servant to sit with all these white guys.

It was like a smack in the face, dad, you know? And that's the thing. I never found a place for myself in this world. I wanted to serve my country. I wanted to make you proud, dad. But here I am, facing charges from the government I spent twelve years working for.

I think you did a brave thing, Byron, says his father. And I am proud of you.

Ya, but that's just it, no one cares. No one cares about those kids in Yemen. I would have been better off just keeping my mouth shut. I faced so much discrimination at work, every single day. And then I get ridiculed by black folks for working for white people. You think that lady who called me a mascot is going to come running, now that I'm facing charges? She doesn't care. Everyone is so damn selfish, dad. This whole fucking world is nothing but assholes looking out for one person, themselves.

There are a lot of things to hate in this world, Byron, says his father. And once you start hating them, and hold onto that hate, it doesn't stop. The world is a wicked place, with lots of suffering, plenty to go around. And hating it feels pretty good. But there's a catch to that hate. Because once you see all of those terrible things, and hate them, and hate the people who cause them, you're going to start seeing all of those terrible things inside yourself. And that hate will turn itself right back onto you.

We all need grace to get through this world. And if you're going to allow yourself grace, you have to give it to others, too. It's only fair. So keep your eye on the good in other people, and in yourself. What you did was right, it doesn't need validation. And if the world punishes you for doing what's right, that's their problem, not yours. You keep doing what's right. You're mother and I are here for you. That's at least two people who care about you.

As the months pass, Byron's anxiety gets worse, and his psychiatrist prescribes him Ambien to help him sleep. He ends up having a severe allergic reaction to it, and has a psychotic episode as a result. He spends a week in the hospital detoxing from the drug, and it takes him several months to recover mentally and emotionally.

Just before his trial, he is offered a plea deal, and he takes it. He gets five years, with the possibility of parole after two. He doesn't remember much of his sentencing hearing, moving through it like a blur. All that he can think about is a vague idea of what prison might be like, a dark and awful thing. He recognizes the faces of his parents in the courthouse, but they seem to register no expression as he passes by them, his hands cuffed before him.

Chapter 7

Byron lies on his bed in the sleeping quarters of the security complex in Baltimore, Maryland. His mattress is seven feet by three and a half feet, just long enough to hold his lengthy frame. To his immediate right is a divider, on the top of which lie a few books. The long room is quiet, filled with the breathing of sleeping men, some of whom call out to phantoms in their dreams.

There are no windows in the room, just a sliver of light that comes through the narrow doorway at the end. Byron feels the nightly press of panic come upon him, and he lets it pass through his chest, out through the ends of his fingertips. His thoughts are tight and spiralled, mimicking the claustrophobia he feels behind the locked walls of the facility.

As he takes a deep breath in through his nose, and lets it out through his mouth, he sees a dark figure at the end of his bed. He sits up, and then the figure turns on a small light that is held in their hand. Through the cone of dim light, Byron can see the face of a young man named Javelle.

You ain't sleeping are you? says Javelle.

No, says Byron. Never. You?

No. I got a test tomorrow I'm trying to pass. They say if I can pass these tests they'll take a few months off my sentence. I was wondering if you might help me out.

Javelle sits down on the bed and shines the little light on the book in his hand. Byron leans over and sees the cover that says Pre–Algebra.

Which part are you wanting to go over? he says.

I don't know. I'm supposed to learn all of it.

We'll let's start at the beginning. You got a paper and a pencil?

Javelle gets out his supplies, and Byron draws out a graph, showing him how to plot points on the x and y axis.

You know about negative numbers? he says. How to add and subtract them?

Ya, I think so.

Just think about it like a credit card account. If you spend fifty dollars with your credit card, you're gonna owe the credit card company fifty dollars, plus interest. That's like the number negative fifty. So you've got negative fifty on your account. Now if you spend fifty more dollars, how much do you owe?

Hundred.

That's right. So that's like negative one hundred. So when you add two negative numbers together, you add them up just like you would positive numbers, only it's a negative total.

They work through the first chapter, and do a few practice problems, and then Javelle shuts his book and stands up.

My brain's full, he says. I can't learn no more of this shit tonight.

Sometimes sleep can help you cement what you've learned into your mind, says Byron. Good luck tomorrow.

I appreciate your help. You seem to really know you're shit. How'd you end up in this place?

I got into bureaucratic trouble with the government.

Like tax fraud?

No. I had access to government secrets that I leaked to the press.

Oh shit. That sounds serious. I thought there was something different about you. Turns out I'm locked up in here with some kind of a James Bond motherfucker.

Ya. Something like that.

Javelle leaves, and Byron lies back down in his bed. The tension in his bones has relieved somewhat, and for the first time in a long time, there is no dull ache at the back of his mind. There is just the pillow on his neck and the mattress on his back. He takes in that moment of peace like he would a cool drink of water. He thinks that if he can find peace on a mattress in prison, he can probably find it anywhere.

Chapter 8

Byron comes out of prison more mature, and his days take on a mellow aroma, neither desperate nor excessive. After two and a half years in lock up, he moves in with his parents, and navigates through each day with a workman's humility. When he lies down at night, and reads a book, he feels peaceful, but he knows that peace will not be there in the morning. Tomorrow will be another day of quiet labor, working towards mental and emotional harmony.

His days become structured into periods of exercise; physical, mental, and emotional. He spends long periods quieting his thoughts, and acknowledging his emotions. At a correctional facility just outside of Houston, he tutors inmates for several hours a week on their high school equivalency classes. On Tuesdays and Thursdays, he participates in a group therapy on how to live well with anxiety.

Byron ends up going out west, to the desert. The isolation suits him. He moves within the windswept landscape, unencumbered by the thorns of the past. The desert scrub dots the dirt around him, and the blackbirds dot the sky above him.

In Ajo, Arizona, he rents a little flat above a gas station, and gets a job filing paperwork for an immigrant advocacy organization. He volunteers with a group that gives aid to migrants passing through the desert. They have a little shed among the scrub where migrants can rest and get information about where to go to apply for asylum.

It is here that Byron spends his long nights, cooking meals for the hungry, assisting with medical aid when it is needed, and ferrying supplies from town. He moves through the atmosphere of desperation and anxiety as one who has experienced it before, thriving like a cactus spike in the harsh desert glare.

On a particularly dark night, the shed is raided by a Border Patrol unit, an elite tactical team that carries heavy weaponry and body armor in steel plated transport trucks. The scene is chaos, and Byron lies on the ground with his hands on his head like the rest of the migrants. Blinding lights sweep the darkness, and rifle barrels thrust out before masked faces.

The group is rounded up and forced into the back of a few vans before anyone is given the chance to speak. Byron finds himself being taken to a Border Patrol holding facility, where the bodies of migrants are stuffed into cages of swollen chain link fencing. He finds an open spot on the concrete floor, and sits down, leaning against the others sitting around him.

One of the backs he leans against belongs to Splint, and Splint turns around to examine the new addition to the holding cell.

Are you an American? says Splint.

Yes, I am, says Byron.

Did you know the Border Patrol can detain anyone it wants to for any reason along the border, even American citizens?

I did know that.

I didn't know that, before I mean. I do now. What'd they detain you for?

I think I'll get a lawyer before I say too much in here.

I understand. My name's Splint. I'm already in trouble. I got charged for manslaughter in the military, and got caught down here at the border. I'm waiting to get taken back to my base for prosecution.

I'm sorry to hear that. I used to be in the Navy, you know. I've been in prison, too.

You have? What's it like?

You remember basic training?

Ya.

Ya. It's about like that. They've got classes you can go through that will help you get out faster. But even after you get out, you're still in the spider's web. Parole, probation, phone calls, soap, it all costs money, and you keep paying even after you get out. It's kind of like empire. You think you're out, but really you're still in the spider's web.

I'm scared shitless of going to jail.

I was too. It took me a long time to adjust. But you do. There's good people in prison, and you'll find them. They'll help you out. You just gotta be ready to help out other people, too.

I'm worried about my dog. I haven't seen her since I got in here.

What's her name?

It's Windy.

I'll see if I can find her at a shelter when I get out of here.

Thank you. I appreciate that.

The next day, a military policeman brings an SUV to the station, in order to take Splint to the airport. Splint gets into the backseat of the SUV, and shuts the door. It has cushioned vinyl upholstery, and he brings the seatbelt across his chest and clicks it into its receptacle. This is the moment he has been waiting for over the last year, to finally face the consequences of his actions. He will now make the long journey north, back across the American plains. All of his progress, no progress at all, in fact. He prays for grace.

About the Author

Christopher Aslan Overfelt lives and works on the empty plains of Kansas. In the summertime he grows cucumbers and in the winters he takes attendance at the local high school. His collection of short stories KANSAS CITY was published by Adelaide Books in 2020.

The novella OUT OF EMPIRE is divided into three parts, and each part follows an American character grappling with their own roles within the American empire, and how to escape it, if possible. The first part takes place across the plains of North America, the second part takes place in Honduras, and the third part takes place in Yemen. Each of these characters interact with other, nonwhite characters, who provide them with perspectives outside of the American empire. Through these journeys, the characters come to terms with their own narratives, and how to live well with themselves, and others.

www.ingramcontent.com/pod-product-compliance
Lightning Source LLC
Chambersburg PA
CBHW021738190726
48288CB00009B/3101